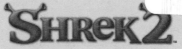

THE MOVIE NOVEL

Adapted by Jesse Leon McCann

Scholastic Inc.

New York Toronto London Auckland Sydney
Mexico City New Delhi Hong Kong Buenos Aires

ISBN: 0-439-53847-5

Published by Scholastic Inc.
SCHOLASTIC and associated logos are trademarks and/or registered trademarks of Scholastic Inc.

12 11 10 9 8 7 6 5 4 3 2 1   4 5 6 7 8 9/0

Designed by Joan Moloney
Printed in the U.S.A.
First printing, May 2004

PROLOGUE

Once upon a time, there lived a beautiful princess named Fiona.

Fiona was no ordinary princess, for a terrible spell had been cast upon her. Every evening as the sun set, Fiona would turn into an ogress and remain that way until dawn. Only true love's first kiss could break the spell.

Acting on the advice of Fiona's Fairy Godmother, Fiona's parents locked her in a distant castle, guarded by a fire-breathing dragon. There the princess waited for a handsome prince to come rescue her.

Sometime later, an ogre named Shrek rescued Fiona from the castle instead. Shrek and his pal, Donkey, accompanied Fiona on a long journey, so she might marry a Lord Farquaad. Farquaad proved to be evil, however, and Fiona and Shrek fell in love with each other. Shrek defeated Farquaad and gave Fiona true love's first kiss. The spell was broken and Fiona became a full-time ogress, day and night. Shrek and Fiona were married and lived happily ever after . . . or did they?

"In his shining suit of armor, Prince Charming rode tirelessly upon his trusty white steed. It was he who would chance the perilous journey through blistering-cold snowstorms and scorching deserts. It was he who would travel for many days and nights, risking life and limb to reach the dragon's keep. For he was the bravest and most handsome in all the land!"

Prince Charming mulled over the words he had just spoken. Yes, his narration had the proper ring to it. He removed his helmet, pulled off his hairnet, and shook out his long, golden locks. He sprayed breath freshener into his mouth.

"And it was destiny that his kiss would break the dreaded curse," Prince Charming said to himself as he entered the ancient castle of the fire-breathing dragon. He didn't notice that there was no dragon in sight.

He ran through the courtyard, past dozens of fallen knights and chunks of dislodged, flame-scorched stone. He climbed countless circular stairways, crossed battle-damaged ramparts, and leapt gaps in broken bridges.

"He alone would climb to the highest room of the tallest tower," the prince proclaimed, finally reaching his destination, slipping into a bedroom full of hanging gowns and undergarments. "To enter the princess's chamber, cross the room to her sleeping silhouette . . ."

Prince Charming approached a shadow slumbering behind the silky drapes of a bed.

". . . and pull back the gossamer curtains to find —" The prince stopped short and gaped. This was *not* what he expected.

In the bed, the Wolf was relaxing.

"What?" asked the Wolf, somewhat put-off at being disturbed.

"Princess Fiona?" the prince inquired nervously.

"No!" Now the Wolf was insulted.

Prince Charming gave a sigh of relief. "Oh, thank goodness! Where is she?"

The Wolf went back to the magazine he'd been reading. "She's on her honeymoon."

"Honeymoon?" cried the dumbfounded prince. "With whom?!"

CHAPTER 1

"Shrek!"

Fiona was concerned that her true love might be hurt. Shrek had stepped into a hunter's rope snare and was now hanging upside down. The ogre's big head kept bobbing in and out of the mud. The offending hunter approached Shrek ominously, while his partner threw a net over Fiona and laughed.

Up until this incident, their honeymoon had been picture-perfect. Well, that is, except for the damage to the Ginger-bread Bed and Breakfast Cottage while Shrek was carrying Fiona over the threshold. Or the moment when they were hugging on the beach, a big wave washed over them, and Shrek ended up kissing a little mermaid. Or the time when the townspeople chased them out of a village with pitch-forks and torches. Or even the unfortunate affair when they scared the dickens out of that Little Red Riding Hood kid — although she *did* leave behind her picnic basket full of good-ies for them to enjoy.

Other than that, though, they'd been having a marvelous honeymoon — shaving side by side in the mornings, making bubbles in the mud bath, doing the happy little things that only two ogres in love could do.

"Hi-yah!" Fiona made short work of the hunter who had thrown the net over her and messed up her 'do. She punched him so hard in the gut, he was down for the count. Then she wrapped the net around the other surprised hunter, swung him around like a sack of potatoes, and sent him flying over the horizon.

"Are you all right, my love?" Fiona asked, running to where Shrek still hung, inverted like some sort of spider-ogre. She wiped the mud from his face and gave him a kiss on his upside-down mouth.

"I am now, Fiona." Shrek grinned. He had never felt so giddy in love with Fiona as he did at that moment. It made his head spin. Either that or the blood was rushing to his brain.

Shrek and Fiona made the perfect couple. Shrek was big, green, and unusual-looking. Fiona was slightly less big, the same shade of green, and much less unusual-looking. Plus, she never complained about how smelly Shrek was. It was a match made in heaven!

But all too soon, their nearly perfect honeymoon was over.

They returned to Shrek's house in the swamp, where

someone had thoughtfully altered the sign to read OGRES —
BEWARE! Once more, Shrek took Fiona into his arms, carried
her giggling over the threshold and into what would now be
their dream cottage, and . . .

. . . the place was a mess. Everything was unkempt or in
shambles. Food containers littered the floors, plants were
dead, the mail was open and left unsorted and scattered.
Even the goldfish were dead, which was strange since Shrek
had never owned any goldfish.

Worst of all, sitting in Shrek's favorite chair, singing to
himself, was the last person in the world that Shrek wanted
to see right then.

CHAPTER 2

"Shrek! Fiona!" cried Donkey, jumping happily out of the chair. "Well, aren't you two a sight for sore eyes! Give us a hug, Shrek, you old love machine!"

Donkey threw his front legs around Shrek and gave him a big bear hug. Donkey then turned to Fiona and presented his muzzle to her for a smooch.

"And look at you, Mrs. Shrek. How about a side of sugar for the steed?"

"Donkey!" Shrek was somewhat miffed. "What are you doing here?"

"I was just taking care of your love nest for you," Donkey replied earnestly.

Shrek eyed the disheveled room again. Uh-huh. Obviously, Donkey hadn't done anything but make a mess.

"Would you look at the time?" Shrek wasn't going to let Donkey ruin their evening. He started pushing Donkey toward the front door. "Well, I guess you'd better be going!"

"Hey, wait a minute! Don't you want to tell me about your trip? Or, how about a game of Parcheesi?" Donkey pushed the other way, doing his best to resist getting invited out. When he wanted to, Donkey could be as stubborn as a mule.

Watching Shrek and Donkey struggle, Fiona said, "Actually, Donkey, shouldn't you be getting home?"

"I thought I'd move back in with you guys!" Donkey said brightly.

Shrek and Fiona looked at each other. Someone was going to have to tell Donkey.

"Well, Donkey, we are always happy to see you . . ." Fiona began helpfully.

"But Fiona and I are married now," Shrek explained. "We need a little time, y'know, to be together . . ."

Donkey stared blankly.

Shrek tried again, "Just with each other . . . *alone*."

"Say no more!" Donkey agreed, taking on the stance of a guard dog. "I will always be here to make sure nobody bothers you!"

"Donkey?" Shrek knew he had to be blunt.

"Yes, roomie?" Donkey said.

"*You're* bothering me."

A dark cloud passed over Donkey's face. Now he got it. His head sagged and he spoke quietly as he slowly backed out the open door.

"Oh, okay. All right, cool. I guess . . . me and Pinocchio

were gonna try and catch a tournament anyway. So, uh, maybe I'll see you Sunday for a barbecue or something . . ."

Donkey disappeared. Fiona looked concerned.

"He'll be fine," Shrek assured her. He smiled and took Fiona into his arms again. "Now, where were we? Oh, I think I remember!"

Shrek began swinging his delighted princess around, dipping her now and again.

Abruptly, Shrek stopped and stared at the door. Donkey was standing there . . . watching. Shrek was so flustered, he accidentally dropped Fiona onto the floor.

"Donkey!"

Donkey was apologetic. "I know, I know! *'Alone.'* I'm going, I'm going!" He turned to leave, but turned back again just before he went through the door. "But what do you want me to tell these other guys?"

Other guys? Puzzled, Shrek and Fiona peeked out the front door.

In front of Shrek's house were dozens of guards.

Shrek sighed, shook his head, and prepared himself for yet another battle. Why couldn't these guards leave an ogre in peace?

All of a sudden, the men in armor formed two lines and made an archway with their spears. Through the arch walked a trumpeter, blowing his horn. After the trumpeter came a dignified page.

The page unrolled his scroll. He spoke in a refined voice.

"'Dearest Fiona, we are so thrilled you finally found your Happily Ever After. Please join us in the kingdom of Far Far Away for a royal ball in honor of your marriage. We can't wait to meet your . . .'"

Here the page stopped and gave Shrek a disdainful once-over before continuing, "'. . . Prince Charming. Love, Mum and Dad.'"

"Mum and Dad?" Fiona was delighted.

"Prince Charming?" Shrek said uneasily.

"Royal ball?" squealed Donkey. "Can I come?"

Shrek frowned. "We're not going!"

Together, Fiona and Donkey gave a horrified, "What?!"

Shrek smiled timidly. "I mean, are we?"

The next morning, their trunks were loaded onto the onion carriage that would take them to the kingdom of Far Far Away. Since everything was in place and ready to go, Donkey grew impatient and jumped on top of the luggage.

"C'mon, Shrek, we don't want to hit traffic!" Donkey yelled at the outhouse. "Shrek!"

Shrek stomped reluctantly out of his house and got into the carriage. Gingerbread Man and other fairy-tale folk were lined up to say good-bye.

"Don't worry! We'll take care of everything!" Gingy

shouted as they all rushed into Shrek's house, slamming the door behind them.

Somehow, that didn't make Shrek feel any better.

The carriage rolled forward. Then, just as the house was out of sight, Shrek heard the sound of breaking glass and loud party music.

No, he wasn't feeling very good about this at all.

CHAPTER 3

The carriage clip-clopped its way over the long, tedious miles. All the while, Donkey asked, "Are we there yet?"

"No," Shrek would grumble.

Through the woods they went, along winding roads, past rural areas, over mountains and bridges.

"Are we there yet?"

"No."

They plodded alongside rivers and through tunnels.

"Are we there yet?"

"No, we are not!" Shrek yelled.

It was tough going for Donkey. He was used to a more active lifestyle.

"I spy with my little eye, something . . . big and shiny!" Donkey tried, hoping Shrek and Fiona would play along. But they frowned and sank lower in their seats — they'd had enough of Donkey talking.

"Shut it, Donkey!" Shrek grumbled sourly.

"But this is taking forever, Shrek!" Donkey pleaded. "And there ain't no in-flight movie or nothing!"

"The kingdom of Far Far Away, Donkey." Shrek gritted his teeth. "That's where we're going, far . . . far . . . away!"

"All right! All right!" Donkey said with chagrin. "I get it. But I'm *really* bored."

"Well, find a way to entertain yourself," Shrek muttered.

For a few moments, the coach was blessed with blissful silence. Fiona and Shrek breathed a concerted sigh of relief for the break in Donkey's chattering. All they could hear was the slow, steady clip-clop of the horses' hooves. The monotonous sound became so relaxing, it almost lulled them to sleep.

"Pop!"

Innocently, Donkey looked at Shrek and Fiona, then out the window and to the floor. Absently, he sucked in his ample lips and released them, making an annoying, wet sound.

"Pop!"

Shrek and Fiona sank lower in their seats with frustration.

"Pop!"

Shrek held his head in his hands.

"Pop!"

"*Arrgghhh!*" Shrek couldn't take it. "For five minutes, could you *not* be yourself, Donkey? For five minutes?"

"Pop!" Donkey replied.

"*Arrrggghhh!* Are we there yet?" cried Shrek.

Fiona gasped excitedly as she glanced out her window. "Yes!"

"Finally!" Donkey exclaimed.

Their carriage rolled into a picture-perfect city. This was fairy-tale central, where dreams came true and the streets were literally paved with golden cobblestones. If you were a young prince or princess, this is where you would settle down in style for your Happily Ever After.

"Wow!" Donkey was in awe. "It's going to be champagne wishes and caviar dreams from now on."

The spectacle outside was so enchanting, Donkey couldn't help but gape with a silly smile on his face.

"Hey, good-looking," Donkey yelled when he saw a beautiful woman walking down the street. "We'll be back to pick you up later!"

Donkey nodded proudly when the woman actually giggled back. What an amazing place! From gilded lampposts to polished marble park benches, everything was lavishly extravagant. They rolled into the business district, passing fine stores, eateries, and boutiques.

The wondrous beauty of the kingdom was not lost on Shrek. "We are definitely *not* in the swamp anymore."

Shrek sat back in his seat, taking it all in. He was clearly overwhelmed by Far Far Away and the prospect of meeting

Fiona's parents. When Fiona saw the look on his face, her own elation subsided a bit. She and Shrek smiled at each other nervously.

Donkey, on the other hand, was having the time of his life! He liked flirting with upper-crust princesses their carriage passed.

"Hi, ladies! Nice day for a parade, huh? Yeah, you workin' that hat!" Donkey chuckled and leaned inside the carriage with a satisfied sigh. "Swimming pools and movie stars!"

In a most elegant neighborhood, the carriage finally rolled to a stop in front of an exquisite castle. A big crowd of anxious locals were gathered, and they let out a cheer when the coachman stepped down from the rig to open the carriage door.

"Announcing the long-awaited return of the beautiful Princess Fiona and her new husband!" a herald proclaimed, and the crowd cheered again.

A red carpet ran from the coach to the castle entrance, and there at the front door stood Fiona's parents. The Queen was beautiful, tall, and elegant, the epitome of regal charm. By contrast, the King had a compact torso, long slender legs, bulging eyes, and a wide mouth.

"Well, this is it," the King said anxiously.

Inside the carriage, Fiona looked at Shrek.

"This is it," she said, putting on a confident smile for his sake.

"This is it," the coachman said, rolling his eyes cynically and opening the carriage door. He'd already seen Shrek and Fiona and knew a disaster was mere seconds away.

The crowd went wild as trumpets sounded. A man standing nearby opened a box and a dozen white doves flew out. Fiona stepped from the coach and the cheering swelled.

Then Shrek stepped out, followed by Donkey.

The trumpets faltered. The crowd's cheers were replaced by gasps. One of the doves was distracted and flew headfirst into the castle wall with a splat. It landed unconscious at the King's feet.

The crowd grew silent. Somewhere, a baby cried.

Donkey looked out at the sea of unhappy faces, gulped, and backed into the carriage again. "Why don't you guys go ahead? I'll park the car."

Shrek and Fiona walked stiffly up the red carpet, smiles plastered on their faces. At the other end of the carpet, Fiona's parents still waved warmly in greeting. Shrek figured they couldn't see them clearly yet.

"So, you still think this is a good idea?" Shrek murmured through clenched teeth.

Not at all sure, but unwilling to admit it, Fiona replied, "Of course. Mom and Dad look happy to see us."

Of course, the smiles on her parents' faces were as big and phony as Shrek's, if not more so.

"Who on earth are they?" the King asked out of the side of his expansive mouth.

"I think that's our little girl," the Queen replied in a shocked whisper.

"That's not little," said the King. "That's a really big problem. Wasn't she supposed to kiss Prince Charming and break the spell?"

The Queen tried to remain upbeat. "Well, he's no Prince Charming, but they do look happy together."

Approaching tentatively, Shrek was far from convinced that things were going okay. Fiona's parents might well be smiling on the outside, but inside they were probably having a fit. Why couldn't Fiona sense it? Perhaps his life as an ogre had made him more aware of people's revulsion, whether they were trying to hide it or not. Fiona was still learning.

"Happy now?" Shrek grinned. "We came. We saw them. Now, let's go before they light the torches."

"They're my parents," Fiona said.

"Hello? They locked you in a tower!"

As his daughter and Shrek drew closer, the King started to sweat. "Now here's our chance, let's go back inside and pretend we're not home."

"Harold!" the Queen admonished. "We have to be polite."

"Quick, while they're not looking!" Shrek urged. "We can make a run for it!"

Fiona poked him. "Shrek! Stop it! Everything's going to be —"

"A disaster!" the King croaked. "There is no way —"

"You can do this," Fiona reassured Shrek.

"But I really want to go!" Shrek assured Fiona.

"Really! Harold!" The Queen nudged the King.

"I want to puke," whispered Shrek.

"I want to puke," whispered the King.

At last, the two couples stood facing each other, all still wearing broad, artificial smiles. Fiona made the first move and ran to embrace her parents. She turned back to her spouse.

"Mom, Dad, I'd like you to meet my husband, Shrek."

Awkward silence.

The King, Queen, and Shrek stood frozen like three grinning statues. Finally, Shrek managed to come up with something to say.

"Well, it's easy to see where Fiona gets her good looks from!" he offered.

CHAPTER 4

Shrek was still grinning when they all sat down for supper that evening. He thought it best to just smile and not say much, until they could get the heck out of there. Still, the silence was deafening. To fill the void, he grabbed a handful of the escargot hors d'oeuvres and popped them into his mouth, shell and all. He crunched loudly as he chewed, making the King shudder in disgust.

Fiona took a drink of her punch, then burped accidentally.

"Excuse me," she said politely.

"Better out than in, I always say, eh, Fiona?" Shrek forgot himself and laughed jovially. "That's good!"

Fiona joined her husband in laughing. The Queen and King, however, were not amused.

Feeling awkward again, Shrek's laughter died abruptly. "Heh, heh . . . guess not."

It was turning out to be the worst dining experience of Shrek's life. He decided to just sit and stare at his silverware until dinner came. That way, his discomfort couldn't possibly get any worse.

Suddenly, there came a disturbance from outside. There was banging and clattering, and someone was yelling at the palace guards.

"What do you mean, I'm not on the guest list?! Don't tell me you don't know who I am!"

Great, thought Shrek. Just what they needed.

Donkey burst through the door and came in. Fiona's parents were horrified.

"Hey, hey, hey!" Donkey greeted them boisterously. "Thanks for waiting. You know, I had the hardest time finding this place!"

Donkey plopped himself down in the chair next to the Queen and gave her a familiar wink.

The King was furious and three burst blood vessels away from a stroke.

"No! No! Bad donkey, bad!" the King scolded. "Down! Down!"

Fiona came to Donkey's rescue. "No! Dad, it's all right! He's with us! He helped rescue me from the dragon!"

The King sat stunned as Donkey tried to regain his composure.

"Yep, that's me, the noble steed!" Donkey brushed himself off and then called out, "Hey, waiter, how about a bowl for the steed?"

"Oh, boy . . ." Shrek said under his breath.

Trying to get past Donkey's unfortunate arrival, Shrek grabbed a spoon and started slurping loudly from a bowl placed in front of him.

"Uh, Shrek?" Fiona said.

"Yah?"

Looking up, Shrek noticed that Fiona was gesturing somewhat urgently at his bowl. Thinking he understood what she was getting at, Shrek nodded knowingly. He turned to Fiona's mom and smiled with all the charm he could muster.

"Oh, sorry. Great soup, Mrs. Q! *Mmmm!*"

Pleased with himself, Shrek went back to his slurping.

Fiona laughed uncomfortably. "No . . . no, darling."

Shrek looked up again, puzzled. Fiona made a big show of dipping her hands into her own finger bowl and then drying them on a cloth. Looking around, Shrek could see that everyone else was doing the same, even Donkey.

"Oh . . . heh, heh . . ." Shrek was abashed. Would this evening *never* end?

Trying to change the subject, the Queen said, "So, Fiona, tell us about where you live."

Fiona smiled proudly at Shrek. "Well, Shrek owns his own land, don't you, honey?"

"Oh, yes," Shrek played along. "It's in an enchanted forest, abundant in squirrels and cute little duckies . . ."

"What?" Donkey interrupted loudly. "Now, I know you ain't talking about the swamp!"

"Donkey!" Shrek pointed one of his little spoons at Donkey, making it seem threatening somehow.

The King rolled his huge, bulbous eyes and said sourly, "An ogre from the swamp. Of course. How original."

Smirking, the King took a sip from his glass. Shrek glared at him but bit down on his tiny spoon rather than offering a snide retort. Boy, he was starting to dislike Fiona's father!

Covering, the Queen said, "Well, I suppose it will be a fine place to raise children."

Startled by the thought, Shrek accidentally sucked the tiny spoon in, and it became lodged in his throat. At the same time, the King choked on his drink and spit out on the table. As Fiona and Donkey looked on worriedly, Shrek started pounding his chest to dislodge the spoon. Finally, he coughed it up and sent it sailing over the table. The Queen tittered uneasily.

"It's a bit early to be thinking about that, isn't it?" Shrek gasped.

"Indeed. I've just started eating!" The King dabbed his chin with a napkin and made a face.

"Harold!" the Queen warned through clenched teeth.

"What's that supposed to mean?" Shrek scowled at the King. Great veins were popping out of the ogre's forehead.

Fiona stepped in to try and calm things. "Dad, it's great, okay?"

The King made a dismissive wave. "Well, for his type, yes."

"My *type*?" Shrek was reaching a boiling point.

Donkey quickly assessed the situation. He knew things were getting out of hand. He had to do something before a fight broke out.

"Uh, I gotta go to the bathroom," Donkey said, and got up to leave.

Just then, an army of servers marched into the dining hall, their arms laden with delicious-smelling food.

"Dinner is served!" announced the Royal Chef.

"Never mind!" Donkey returned to his place. "I can hold it."

For the moment, the squabbling was forgotten as the servers laid out a spread of all manner of delicacies.

"Bon appétit!" said the Chef.

"*Mmm*! Mexican food!" Donkey licked his lips. "My favorite!"

They dug in, but the undeclared truce between Shrek and the King didn't last.

The King grabbed an entire lobster and eyeballed Shrek.

"So, I suppose any grandchildren I could expect from you would be . . . ?" the King began.

"Ogres, yes!" Shrek angrily grabbed the carcass of a cooked goose.

"Not that there's anything wrong with that, right, Harold?" the Queen interjected.

The King brought up a sharp knife and slammed it into the lobster's shell, ripping it in half and glaring at Shrek as if he wished Shrek were the lobster.

"Oh, no, of course not," the King answered peevishly. "That is, assuming you don't eat your own young."

Fiona was getting really annoyed. "Dad . . ."

Shrek savagely pulled the legs off his goose, allowing the body to fall back on his plate with a thud.

"No, we usually prefer the ones who've been locked away in a *tower*," Shrek said sarcastically.

"Shrek, please!" Fiona's face was flushed with anger.

"I only did that because I love her!" The King stabbed a piece of beef with a fondue fork and stared daggers at Shrek.

"Oh, aye! Day care or dragon-guarded castle?!" Shrek ripped open the goose with his bare hands to let the stuffing out.

"You wouldn't understand!" The King cracked open a lobster claw violently. "You're not her father!"

Things escalated from there. Shrek began choking his goose's neck. The King responded by tearing the meat out of the back of his lobster. Shrek returned fire, squeezing a banana from its peel. Countering, the King crushed a handful of crackers. Shrek smashed some walnuts with his fist. The King irately ground some pepper. Shrek broke a wishbone in half. The King beheaded a fish.

"It's so nice to have the family together for dinner," the Queen said, trying desperately to salvage the situation.

Simultaneously, the King and Shrek grabbed for the roasted pig in the center of the table. They each seized a spit prong and pulled up as hard as they could. The pig was heaved high into the air.

"Harold!" The Queen was shocked.

"Shrek!" Fiona was furious.

"Fiona!" replied Shrek defensively.

"Fiona!" the King roared.

"Mom!" Fiona cried.

"Harold!" the Queen implored.

"Donkey!" Donkey figured he might as well get into the game.

SLAM!

The pig landed heavily on the table, and the room fell silent. They all stared at one another, stunned. Fiona buried her face in her hands. She ran out of the room sobbing, leaving the King and Shrek to glare at each other. Everything became deathly quiet.

CHAPTER 5

Back in her room, Fiona tried to pinpoint exactly why she was so upset. Well, it was obvious, wasn't it? She was crying because Shrek and her father weren't getting along.

No. That wasn't quite it.

Actually, she was upset because her parents would never fully accept Shrek as their son-in-law. Yes, that was the truth of the matter.

No, no. It was something more.

If her parents didn't accept the ogre she loved, that meant they really didn't accept *her*. That was the heart of it, and it was hard for her to take.

Fiona stepped out onto her balcony for some fresh air. She looked at the twinkling lights of the kingdom, and the sight made her sadder. All those people, in all the houses and cottages — they would shun Shrek *and* her for the rest of their days.

She bent her head and closed her eyes. A single teardrop

ran down her cheek and dropped off her chin. She opened her eyes and watched the teardrop fall, almost in slow motion. When it hit the railing, a beautiful musical note sounded.

Puzzled, she looked around. What in the world was that?

Her eyes fell upon a bubble dropping from above — quietly like a whisper. When the bubble was right in front of her, it popped and made a musical tone, too. Another bubble dropped from above, then another and another. Soon the air around her was filled with bubbles, and each time they popped, a different note played, creating an enchanting melody.

Finally, a much larger bubble floated down. Inside it was an older woman with glasses, a motherly smile, and flapping wings sparkling with fairy dust. As the bubble music played, the woman sweetly sang.

"Your fallen tears have called to me,
So here comes my sweet remedy,
I know what every princess needs,
For her to live life happily!"

Her woes temporarily forgotten, Fiona laughed. The woman's bubble popped and she stepped onto Fiona's balcony amid a chorus of sweeping harp music.

The woman turned to smile at Fiona, and uttered a little shriek. "Look at you! You're all . . . grown up," she finally said.

"Who are you?" Fiona asked.

The woman smiled ever-so-sweetly, closed her eyes, and did a little curtsy. "Oh, sweet pea. I'm your Fairy Godmother!"

Fiona was surprised. "I have a Fairy Godmother?"

"Now don't worry. I'm here to make it all better," the Fairy Godmother said, walking around Fiona, looking her up and down. Fiona was surprised to see that she had a disapproving — even shocked — look on her face.

With a wave of the Fairy Godmother's wand, the room came alive. Inanimate objects started moving. Out of nowhere, a cheerful tune began to play. Much to her dismay, Fiona realized a musical number had started.

The Fairy Godmother sang:

"With just a wave of my magic wand,
Your troubles will soon be gone,
With a flick of the wrist and just a flash,
You'll land a prince with a ton of cash!"

"Excuse me, I . . ." Fiona began.

The revelers in her room weren't listening. Now her chamber pot was actually doing a jig. The Fairy Godmother continued her song:

"A high-priced dress made by mice no less,
Some crystal glass pumps and no more stress,
Your worries will vanish, your soul will cleanse."

The chest of drawers joined the Fairy Godmother, singing in harmony:

"Confide in your very own furniture friends,
We'll help you set a new fashion trend."

An enchanted chair flew over, knocking Fiona off her feet. The Fairy Godmother didn't seem to notice, she just kept on singing:

"I'll make you fancy,
I'll make you great,
The kind of gal a prince would date,
They'll write your name near the phone on the wall . . ."

In a deep bass, the mirror crooned:

"For a happy ever after, give Fiona a call!"

After this, the number got wilder. The music became more frenzied and objects danced crazily across the floor or through the air. A brush tried to fix Fiona's hair. Makeup tried to apply itself to her face. She kept batting objects away because it was all rather unnerving. The Fairy Godmother didn't seem to notice. She kept singing and dancing. At one point, she conjured up a little dog, a bichon frise, and put it in Fiona's arms, as if to appease her. Fiona had to hold the dog out at arm's length because it was licking her all over.

Eventually, the whole production number came to an abrupt halt when Shrek and Donkey crashed into the room, drawn by all the noise.

"Fiona!" exclaimed Shrek.

Everyone and everything gasped at Shrek in horror.

"Oh, my gosh! You've got a puppy!" Donkey cried.

"Shrek!" Fiona said, embarrassed, straightening her hair. "Ah, Fairy Godmother, I'd like you to meet my husband . . . Shrek."

The Fairy Godmother was appalled and her fairy wings flapped with agitation. "Your *husband*? What? When did this happen?"

"Shrek is the one who rescued me," Fiona explained.

"But that can't be right!" the Fairy Godmother exclaimed.

"Please, don't be offended." Shrek said irritably. "It was a small ceremony."

"Shrek!" Fiona frowned. "She's just trying to help."

"Good, she can help us pack," Shrek said, turning back to Fiona. "Get your coat, dear, we're leaving!"

"What?" Fiona exclaimed.

"Leaving?" Donkey cried. This was news to him.

"When did you decide this?" Fiona asked.

"Shortly after arriving," Shrek replied.

"Look . . . I'm sorry . . ." Fiona said, turning back to the Fairy Godmother and trying to apologize.

"No, that's all right. I need to go anyway." The Fairy Godmother pushed her glasses up on her nose and pulled out a business card. "If you should ever need me, happiness is just a teardrop away."

Shrek snatched the card away before Fiona could.

"Thanks, but we've got all the happiness we need," Shrek said with a phony grin. "Happy, happy, happy!"

"Oh, I see, heh, heh," the Fairy Godmother replied agreeably.

With a wave of her wand, she returned all the inanimate objects to their rightful places. When everything was back to normal, the Fairy Godmother stepped out to the balcony and disappeared into a flying carriage waiting for her there. Only the dog remained, drooling happily.

Fiona gave Shrek the evil eye. "Very nice, Shrek."

"What?" Shrek scowled. "I told you coming here was a bad idea."

Fiona crossed her arms. "Do you think it might be nice if someone asked me what I wanted?"

"Oh, sure . . . do you want me to pack for you?" Shrek asked, sarcastically.

"You're unbelievable! You're behaving like . . ." Fiona began, then stopped herself.

"Bark! Bark!" The little bichon frise joined the conversation.

"Go on, say it!" Shrek demanded.

"Bark! Bark! Bark!" the dog replied.

"Like an ogre!" Fiona yelled.

Getting into her face, Shrek said, "Well, here's a news flash for ya — whether your parents like it or not — I *am* an ogre!"

"Bark! Bark! Bark!"

Shrek turned his attention to the little dog and snarled, *"RRRROAR!"*

The dog stopped barking and wet itself.

"And guess what, *Princess*?" Shrek said firmly. "That's not going to change."

"I've made changes for *you*, Shrek. Think about that," Fiona said, quietly.

With a heavy heart, she went to the door and slammed it behind her. Shrek stood in stunned silence.

"Real smooth, Shrek," Donkey scolded from the corner where he'd been watching. "I'm an ogre — *ROAR!*"

Shrek moved to follow Fiona, but stopped at her door and listened. From the other side, he could hear her crying. He stood there with his hand on the door handle, not sure what to do.

CHAPTER 6

Meanwhile, the King and Queen overheard Shrek and Fiona's argument.

"I knew this would happen!" The King was beside himself, hopping about the room and ranting.

"You should," the Queen replied simply. "You started it."

The King made an indignant face. "I can hardly believe *that*, Lillian! He's the ogre, not me."

The Queen tried to bring things down a notch, saying soothingly, "Harold, you're taking this a little too personally. This is Fiona's choice."

At first the King was charmed. But he grew uneasy again and paced away with a worried frown.

"Yes, but she was supposed to choose the prince we picked out for her! You expect me to give my blessings to this . . . this thing?"

The Queen continued, "Fiona does. And she'll never forgive you if you don't. I don't want to lose your daughter again, Harold. . . . You act as if love is totally predictable.

Don't you remember when we were young? We used to walk by the lily pond."

"It was where we had our first kiss." The King was momentarily lost in the memory. It had been a happier time, before he had to worry about daughters and ogres.

Then the thought of the current situation returned the fire to his eyes.

"It's not the same! I don't think you realize that our daughter has married a monster!"

"Stop being such a drama King!" The Queen sighed.

The King didn't like being made fun of. His large eyes grew wider and he did a sarcastic little dance.

"Fine, fine! Pretend there's nothing wrong! La-dee-da-dee-da! Isn't it all wonderful?"

He stalked toward the balcony in a huff, leaving her in the bedroom. They'd been married long enough for her to know that when he was like this, only the passing of time would calm him. As the King stepped out onto his balcony, he was met by a disagreeable voice.

"Hello, Harold."

"*Ahhh!*" the King shouted.

The Fairy Godmother was seated in the back of her magical floating carriage, parked just off the balcony railing. Since they were several hundred feet up, the King hadn't exactly expected anyone to come calling.

"What happened?" asked the Queen from inside.

The King stuck his head back into the chamber. He held the balcony drapes close to his body, so the Queen didn't see he had a visitor.

"Nothing, dear!" He smiled falsely. "Just the old crusade wound playing up a bit! Ha-ha! Ahh . . . I'll just stretch it out here for a while."

The King backed out again, shutting the drapes carefully. He dreaded to hear what the Fairy Godmother wanted. He couldn't help thinking that it would be something inconvenient. Hadn't he had enough trouble for one day?

"You better get in," the Fairy Godmother said, sweetly patting the seat in the coach next to her. "We need to talk."

"Actually, Fairy Godmother, I'm just off to bed. I've already taken my pills, and they tend to make me a bit drowsy." The King began to edge away, hoping to get back into the safety of his castle. "So, how about . . ."

The King backed into something hard. Two of the Fairy Godmother's goons had moved in behind him. They were huge and about as solid as the Third Little Pig's brick house. They stared down at him with cold eyes.

". . . we make this a quick visit, eh?"

Intimidated, the King hopped quickly into the flying carriage and the goons followed. As soon as everyone was seated, the carriage flew off into the night. The Fairy Godmother pulled the carriage drapes shut, making the interior seem more suffocating to the King.

"So, what's new?" The King smiled, trying to look relaxed.

"You remember my son, Prince Charming?" The Fairy Godmother gestured.

The King noticed Prince Charming for the first time. The prince sat with his arms crossed, his perfect nose stuck into the air, and a pout on his handsome face.

"Charming? Is that you! My gosh, it's been years! Wh-wh-when did you get back?" the King stammered.

"Oh . . . about five minutes ago," Prince Charming said, looking at his watch disdainfully. "After I endured blistering winds and scorching desert! I climbed to the highest room in the tallest tower —"

The Fairy Godmother intervened, patting her son softly on his broad chest.

"Charming, sweetheart, Mummy can handle this." The Fairy Godmother turned to frown at the King. "He endures blistering winds and scorching desert! He climbs to the highest room in the tallest tower, and what does he find? A trespassing wolf telling him that his princess — your daughter — is already married!"

The King swallowed hard. "Well, what can I do? I mean, it wasn't *my* fault he didn't get there in time."

"Stop the car!" the Fairy Godmother screeched. "Harold, you force me to do something I really don't want to do."

The goons cracked their knuckles. Filled with fear and apprehension, the King broke out in a swampy sweat.

"Where are we?"

In answer, the Fairy Godmother gave a little smile and opened the drape and window on her side. Outside was another window, with a pimple-faced teenager standing in it.

"Hi there!" said the teen enthusiastically. "Welcome to Friar's Fat Boy! May I take your order?"

"My diet is ruined! I hope you're happy!" the Fairy Godmother told the King while scanning the menu. "Okay, two Renaissance Wraps, *no mayo*, chili rings . . ."

"I'll have a Medieval Meal . . ." Prince Charming added.

"Harold, curly fries?" the Fairy Godmother asked the King.

"Uh, no thank you," the King replied.

"Sourdough Soft Taco, then?" She raised her eyebrows. "What do you want?"

"Nothing, really. I'm fine."

"Here's your order, Fairy Godmother!" the teen said presently, handing over a sack. "And this comes with the Medieval Meal!"

The Friar's Fat Boy employee lugged a heavy battle-ax up to the window and passed it through to the Fairy Godmother with wobbling arms.

"Here you are, dear." The Fairy Godmother handed the battle-ax to a delighted Prince Charming, who had been digging through his meal, searching for his prize.

The carriage swept up into the night sky again and left the fast-food drive-thru behind.

The Fairy Godmother sorted through her dinner sack. "We made a deal, Harold. And I assume you don't want me to go back on my part?" The Fairy Godmother looked at the King pointedly.

The King croaked, "Indeed not!"

The Fairy Godmother leaned closer, looming like a tiger. "So Fiona and Charming *will* be together?"

"Yes." The King's eyes bugged out.

This seemed to appease the Fairy Godmother. She sat back, sighed, and then looked at her son fondly.

"Oh, believe me, Harold. It's what's best . . ." the Fairy Godmother said.

The King took his eyes off the Fairy Godmother and focused on her boy. Prince Charming was trying on the paper crown that came with his meal. He smiled at the King.

"Well, what am I supposed to do about it?" the King asked, turning back to the Fairy Godmother.

The carriage came to a screeching stop back outside the King's balcony. He swiftly and gratefully stepped out.

The Fairy Godmother grabbed the Medieval Meal battle-ax from an obviously disappointed Prince Charming and threw it to the King.

"Use your imagination!" the Fairy Godmother commanded.

The door slammed shut and the carriage flew away, leaving the forlorn King alone on his balcony, holding the battle-ax. Kill Shrek? The King didn't know if he had it in him. Then again, the alternative was much, much worse. He sadly watched the carriage disappearing into the distance. Just as it faded out of sight, he heard the Fairy Godmother's fearsome voice, carried over the cool night air.

"There's *mayo* on this Renaissance Wrap!"

CHAPTER 7

The day had disappeared. The forest quickly turned from a pleasant friendly place to a claustrophobic, forbidding place. Gnarled tree branches seemed like twisted fingers that would reach down and snatch them at any moment.

Donkey shuddered. He could hardly believe they were only a few miles from the bustling metropolis of Far Far Away.

All at once, Shrek stopped and said, "Face it, Donkey. We're lost."

"We can't be lost," Donkey replied, more from nerves than actual confidence. "We followed the King's instructions exactly. What did he say? 'Head to the deepest, darkest part of the woods . . .'"

"Aye," Shrek agreed.

"'Past the sinister trees with those scary-looking branches . . .'" Donkey continued.

"Check."

Donkey pointed. "Yeah, and there's that bush shaped like an hourglass."

"We passed that bush three times already!" Shrek was frustrated.

"Hey, you were the one who didn't want to stop and get directions!" Donkey reminded him.

"Oh, great!" Shrek threw his arms up into the air. "My one chance to fix things with Fiona's dad, and I end up lost in the woods with you!"

"All right, you don't have to get huffy!" Donkey said defensively. "I'm only trying to help."

"I know!" Shrek yelled. Then he sighed with a deep breath.

Donkey was right. Shrek shouldn't blame him for the lousy situation he was in. Donkey didn't cause his argument with Fiona the previous evening. And it was Shrek who decided to take the King up on his offer to meet for a morning hunt.

Shrek thought back to the events of the night before.

Fiona had gone to bed after they'd somewhat made up. But as she snored softly . . . well, softly for an ogre, anyway, he was still restless and irritated. He sat on the bed, surrounded by reminders of Fiona's childhood.

He got up and watched the lights of the Far Far Away sign on the side of a nearby mountain. Would Fiona be happier living here? He wandered over to a shelf filled with Fiona's old toys and spotted her hope chest on the bureau.

Checking that Fiona was still asleep, he carefully opened the chest and quickly removed her diary. He flipped it open to a place near the beginning.

Dear Diary,

Sleeping Beauty is having a slumber party tomorrow, but Dad says I can't go.
He never lets me out after sunset.

It bothered Shrek that Fiona suffered at an early age because of her curse. He flipped the diary to a page farther in.

Dear Diary,

Dad says I'm going away for a while. It must be a finishing school or something.

Poor kid. That was when she was about to be sent to the tower. He flipped a few more pages. Fiona's penmanship got substantially better, more mature.

Dear Diary,

Mom says that when I'm old enough, my handsome Prince Charming will rescue me from my tower and bring me back to my family! And we'll all live happily ever after!

So, as she sat waiting in the tower, young Fiona had a clear idea of the kind of man she wanted to marry someday.

The thought brought out mixed emotions in him. It didn't make him feel very confident to realize that he was nothing like the handsome prince that young Fiona was hoping for. Uneasily, he flipped to another page.

Dear Diary,

Mrs. Fiona Charming. Mrs. Fiona Charming. Mrs. Fiona Charming. Mrs. Fiona Charming. Mrs. Fiona Charming. Mrs. Fiona Charming. Mrs. Fiona Charming. Mrs. Fiona Charming. Mrs. Fiona Charming. Mrs. Fiona Charming. Mrs. Fiona Charming. Mrs. Fiona Charming. Mrs. Fiona Charming. Mrs. Fiona Charming. Mrs. Fiona Charming. Mrs. Fiona Charming. Mrs. Fiona Charming. Mrs. Fiona Charming. Mrs. Fiona Charming . . .

Nope, it didn't make him feel very confident at all. Shrek skipped ahead several pages.

Mrs. Fiona Charming. Mrs. Fiona Charming. Mrs. Fiona Charming. Mrs. Fiona Charming. Mrs. Fiona Charming. Mrs. Fiona Charming. Mrs. Fiona Charming. Mrs. Fiona Charming. Mrs. Fiona Charming . . .

Shrek broke out in a cold sweat.

The tension in his body was like a tightly wound spring, so when someone tapped on their door, he jumped like a water drop on a hot plate. He quickly stashed the diary back into the chest and checked to see if the knocking had awakened Fiona. When he was certain she was still asleep, Shrek cracked open the door to see who it was.

The smiling King greeted him, "Ah! I hope I'm not interrupting anything."

Shrek opened the door a little wider. "No, I was just reading a scary book."

"Yes, well, listen . . ." the King said. "I was hoping you'd let me apologize for my behavior earlier."

Shrek raised an eyebrow. "Okay?"

"I don't know what came over me," the King continued. "Do you suppose we could just pretend it never happened and start over?"

Shrek didn't know what to think. This was unexpected. Shrek's natural tendency was to not trust others, so he figured the best thing to do was to put the King off until Fiona was awake.

"Look, Your Majesty . . ." Shrek began.

The King's wide mouth smiled wider. "Please! Call me Dad."

"Dad," Shrek continued awkwardly. "We both acted like ogres, maybe we just need some time to get to know each other."

"Excellent idea!" The King gave a happy hop. "I was actually hoping you might join me in the woods for a morning hunt. A little father-son time?"

Now, this was totally outside Shrek's frame of reference. Father-son time?

"I know it would mean the world to Fiona," the King urged from the other side of the door.

That had done it. If it meant that Fiona would be happier, Shrek couldn't possibly say no. And what harm could it do? Shrek would make nice with Fiona's dad, spend some "quality" time, and then he and Fiona could return to their swamp in peace.

So Shrek had agreed to meet the King in the deep, dark forest the following morning. Now he and Donkey were hopelessly lost in woods that were becoming creepier by the second.

But Shrek knew it wasn't Donkey's fault, and he felt bad about casting blame on his long-eared friend.

As dead leaves swept past their feet, Shrek said in a softened voice, "I'm sorry, all right?"

"Hey, don't worry about it," Donkey pouted.

"I just really need to make things work with this guy," Shrek explained earnestly.

Donkey looked closely at Shrek. The big guy was really trying to do the right thing. As mean as Shrek could be sometimes, Donkey could never stay mad at him for long.

"Ah, sure." Donkey smiled. "Now, let's go bond with Daddy."

They continued on, two friends smiling, happy to be on

good terms again. So focused on each other that they didn't notice a pair of eyes gazing at them from the shadows. Fierce eyes. Predator's eyes.

"Purrrrrrr!" came a sound.

"Well, well, well, Donkey!" Shrek grinned. "I know it was kind of a tender moment back there, but the purring?"

Donkey looked up, scowling, "Man, what are you talking about? I ain't purring."

Shrek snickered, "Oh, sure. What's next? A hug?"

"Shrek, donkeys don't purr," Donkey protested. "What do you think I am?"

As silent as poison, the creature that stalked them moved through the underbrush. Like a blur, it jumped into their path and hissed angrily. Startled, Shrek and Donkey stopped in their tracks.

"Ha-ha!" the creature sneered. "Fear me, if you dare! Hissss!"

Once Upon a Time...

Prince Charming
arrives to rescue
the fair princess.

But she's already left
for her honeymoon,
the Wolf explains.

The Journey to Far Far Away . . .

"Are we there yet?"

"Yes, we are!"

Meeting the In-laws . . .

"We're definitely not in the swamp anymore."

Fiona's parents meet her Prince Charming.

A Peaceful Family Dinner . . .

Maybe things will be better after we eat.

Later that night Shrek explores Fiona's childhood room.

Mrs Fiona Charming

Every Princess Has a Fairy Godmother...

The Fairy Godmother always has the perfect spell for any situation.

It never hurts to advertise.

HAPPINESS

Fear Me...If You Dare

The Ogre Hunter, Puss In Boots.

"How many cats can wear boots? Honestly? Let's keep him!"

A Little Potion Magic...

Shrek is a new man — a very handsome one.

"Who are you calling Donkey?"

To the castle!

Shrek and Fiona finally get their happy ending.

CHAPTER 8

After a momentary fright, Shrek smiled and relaxed. "Hey, look! A little cat."

It was true. A cat stood before them in a defiant stance. It wore leather boots up to its thighs, a cape, and a feathered musketeer hat. It stared at them piercingly. Shrek wasn't afraid, but Donkey didn't like the sword the cat was brandishing.

"Look out, Shrek! He's got a piece!"

"It's a cat, Donkey!" Shrek crouched down playfully. "Ohhh, c'mere, little kitty, kitty, kitty! C'mon. C'mere, little kitty."

When Shrek moved a little closer, the cat leapt out of its boots and dived right at the ogre. It landed on Shrek's thigh and clamped its claws deeply into his flesh.

"Ahhhh!" Shrek was painfully surprised.

"Meowrrrl!" the cat growled, crawling its way into Shrek's shirt, then tearing its way out again.

In tremendous pain, Shrek grabbed for the energetic feline, but missed. The cat reattached itself to his thigh with an excruciating ripping sound. Shrek screamed in agony.

"Hold on, Shrek! I'm coming!" Donkey hastened to aid his friend.

"Get it off! Get it off! Get it off!" Shrek cried. "Ohhhh!"

Donkey tried to bat the cat off, but only managed to kick Shrek instead.

"Hold still, Shrek! Hold still!"

As Shrek hopped around in pain and Donkey fumbled, the cat leapt stealthily over the ogre's back, landing back on the trail in its boots. With a deft slash of its sword, the cat carved a "P" in a nearby tree and turned back to them with a flourish.

"Now, ye ogre, pray for mercy from . . . Puss In Boots!" the cat announced in a thick Spanish accent.

"Oohh, I'll kill that cat!" Shrek thundered, approaching the cat with his fists raised.

Puss merely laughed with bravado. He pointed his sword and took an attack stance. But just as Puss and Shrek were about to come to blows, the cat faltered. His eyes went wide. He stumbled and dropped his sword. Puss grabbed his throat.

"Ack! Gack!" the cat choked.

The cat dropped to the ground, his body writhing in spasms. A moment later he coughed up a huge chunk of something, and it splattered on the ground.

"Heh, heh . . . hair ball." Puss smiled sheepishly, getting to his feet.

Donkey was grossed out. "Oh! That is nasty!"

As Puss was distracted, Shrek took the opportunity to pick him up by the scruff of the neck.

"Ah!" Puss struggled harmlessly in the ogre's powerful grip.

"What do ya reckon we should do with him?" Shrek asked Donkey.

Donkey grinned evilly. "I say we take that sword and neuter him right here!"

"Oh, madre!" Puss cried. "No, por favor! I implore you. It was nothing personal, señor. I was doing it for my family. My mother, she is sick, and my father lives off the garbage! The King offered me much in gold, and I have a litter of brothers and . . ."

"Whoa, whoa, whoa!" Shrek stopped him. "Fiona's father paid you to kill me?"

"The rich King?" Puss nodded. "Sí."

Shrek set Puss on the ground and stalked away. "Well, so much for 'one big, happy family.'"

"C'mon, Shrek, don't feel bad." Donkey followed his pal. "Almost everybody that meets you wants to kill you."

"Gee, thanks," Shrek grumbled. "Would Fiona have been better off if I were really some sort of Prince Charming?"

"That is what the King said," Puss answered.

Shrek and Donkey turned. They gave him icy glares.

"Oh, sorry," Puss said. "I thought the question was directed at me."

"It's not like I wouldn't change if I could." Shrek resumed walking.

Donkey laughed. "Into a prince? Now, that would take some kind of miracle!"

A miracle? That gave Shrek an idea.

"Hold the phone!" Shrek exclaimed, pulling the Fairy Godmother's business card out of his pocket. Any Fairy Godmother worth her salt should be able to transform him into a prince.

The card read "Happiness is just a teardrop away."

That was a problem. Shrek never cried. But, he thought, maybe he could get Donkey to.

"Donkey, think of the saddest thing that's ever happened to you," Shrek said.

Donkey thought for a second, then pursed his lips angrily. "Aw, man, where do I begin? Well, first there was the time the old farmer tried to sell me for some magic beans. I ain't never got over that. Then this fool went off and had a party, and he had all the guests trying to pin the tail on me! Then they started beating me with a stick and going 'Piñata! Piñata!' What is a piñata, anyway?"

"No, Donkey." Shrek closed his eyes wearily. "I need you to cry."

"Yeah, well, don't go projecting on me," Donkey scoffed. "I know you're feeling bad, but you gotta let your own . . . Uggggggggh!"

While Donkey was carrying on, Puss came over and stepped on his hoof with the sharp heel of his boot. Donkey let out a cry, and Shrek quickly held the card under him. Sure enough, a tear came to Donkey's eye and dropped onto the business card.

Donkey looked at Puss and muttered, "Hairy, litter-licking sack of —"

But he was interrupted when a glowing bubble appeared before them. Inside was the Fairy Godmother, smiling sweetly in her old-lady glasses, her fairy wings beating rhythmically.

"This is Fairy Godmother. I'm either away from my desk or with a client."

Darn! This must be her answering service.

"But if you come by the office, we'll be glad to make you a personal appointment. Have a happy ever after."

With that, the bubble popped and the image of the Fairy Godmother disintegrated. Shrek and Donkey exchanged amazed looks.

"Whoa," Donkey said.

Shrek smiled. "Are you up for a little quest, Donkey?"

"All right!" Donkey cheered happily. "That's more like it! Shrek and Donkey, on another whirlwind adventure!"

Donkey was so excited, he started singing, "Ain't no stopping us now! Whoo! We're on the move!"

"Stop!" Puss interrupted, looking sincerely at Shrek. "Ogre, I have misjudged you."

"Join the club," Shrek replied. "We've got jackets."

Puss bowed earnestly. "On my honor, I am obliged to accompany you until I have saved your life as you have spared mine."

Donkey frowned and shook his head. "I'm sorry, the position of annoying talking animal has already been taken. Let's go, Shrek."

Donkey moved off haughtily. After a bit, he realized that Shrek wasn't with him.

"Shrek?" Donkey turned to find Shrek smiling down at Puss. "Shrek!"

Donkey was horrified. Puss was sitting on the ground and looking up at Shrek with his big, innocent cat eyes. And Shrek was falling for it, hook, line, and sinker!

"Aw, c'mon, Donkey," Shrek said. "Look at him, in his wee little boots. You know, how many cats can wear boots? Honestly? Let's keep him!"

"Say what?" Donkey cried.

Now both Puss and Shrek were giving Donkey the soulful-eyes routine. Donkey, exasperated and knowing there was no hope of winning, didn't even put up an argument.

"Aarrrrghh!" Donkey exclaimed, and marched away.

"Oooh, listen!" Shrek was carrying Puss. "He's purring."

"Oh, so now it's cute?" Donkey scoffed.

"Aw, c'mon, Donkey, lighten up," Shrek said, gently scratching Puss under his chin.

"Lighten up?" Donkey laughed at the irony, as the trio passed out of the dark woods and over a hill. "Oh, I should lighten up? Look who's telling who to lighten up!"

CHAPTER 9

Back at the castle, preparations were under way for the royal ball. It was going to be a fairy-tale affair, a glittering event in the making. The Queen surveyed the progress, making sure everything was absolutely perfect. The King followed her, lost in thought. Several servants surrounded the Queen, each carrying items that would be seen, used, or consumed at the ball.

The Queen studied fabric swatches a servant held up to her. "Hmmm . . . they're both festive, aren't they?" She turned to the King. "What do you think, Harold?"

"Very good, fine . . . mmm," the King mumbled, not looking up.

"Try to at least *pretend* that you're interested in your daughter's wedding ball!"

"Honestly, Lillian, I don't think it really matters," protested the King. "How do we know there's even going to be a ball?"

The Queen looked at him suspiciously. Oops! Had he

said too much? He didn't want to tip her off. Hopefully, the ogre hunter had done his job by then.

"Mom! Dad!"

Fiona provided a much-needed distraction.

"Oh, hello, dear!" The Queen smiled warmly at her daughter.

The King didn't waste the opportunity to escape. He looked up and pretended one of the servants was asking for him on the other side of the expansive ballroom.

"Uh, what's that, Cedric? Right! Coming!" The King hopped off while the Queen's attention was on Fiona.

Fiona looked worried. When she'd woken earlier, she found that Shrek was gone. Was he still angry? She'd thought they had sort of made up after their tiff.

"Mom, have you seen Shrek?" Fiona asked as she approached the Queen.

"I haven't," the Queen replied as she studied the servant's samples of fabric. "You should ask your father."

Fiona followed after her father. The Queen had a sudden thought, turned, and called to her. "Be sure to use small words, dear. He's a little slow this morning."

Aware that Fiona was approaching, the King attempted to look busy. If he convinced her that he'd been helping with the ball preparations, it would make sense that he wouldn't have a clue as to Shrek's whereabouts. Besides, he needed to focus on something other than his daughter's face. He found that when he looked at Fiona too closely, his ability to lie to her was diminished considerably.

The King walked next to Cedric, a kitchen hand who was carrying a big bowl filled with some sort of chopped meat.

"Can I help you, Your Majesty?" Cedric asked, puzzled by the King's sudden attention.

"Dad?" Fiona had caught up with him.

"Ah, yes . . . hmmm!" The King stuck his fingers in Cedric's bowl, scooped up some of the meat, and ate it. "Exquisite! What do you call this dish?"

"That would be the dog's breakfast, Your Majesty."

"Ah, yes." The King smiled sheepishly. "Very good, then. Carry on, Cedric."

The King headed off, not looking at his daughter.

Fiona followed after him. "Dad, have you seen Shrek?"

The King pretended to think hard for a moment, then said, "Ah, no, I haven't, dear."

"It's not like him to leave without saying anything."

"I wouldn't worry, dear." The King patted her shoulder. "I'm sure he just went off to look for a nice mud hole to cool down in after your little spat last night."

"Oh, you heard that, huh?" Fiona gave an apologetic smile.

"Darling, the *whole* kingdom heard that." The King had to rub it in. "I mean, after all, it is in his nature to be, well, a bit of a brute."

"Him?" Fiona wouldn't let her father start dissing Shrek again. "You didn't exactly roll out the welcome wagon."

"Well, what did you expect?" The King was defensive. "I mean look at what he's done to you."

"Shrek loves me for who I am," she said simply. "I would think you could be happy for me."

Oh, it broke his heart to see her like this. After all, she was his little girl and he did love her dearly — even if her present appearance was not what he had hoped for. He put his arm around her.

"Darling, I'm just thinking about what's best for you," the King said. "You're a princess. You deserve so much better than this."

The King left her then. Fiona felt more confused than ever.

CHAPTER 10

After walking many miles, Shrek, Donkey, and Puss came to the clearing where the Fairy Godmother's cottage was located. It was a pretty spot, with a happy garden in front and a freshly painted little fence surrounding it. It was the kind of place in which one might expect a kindly older woman to reside.

Behind the cute cottage, however, was a massive factory with several smokestacks filling the air with billowing magical soot. A cacophony of loud, clanking machines could be heard inside. Colorful waste product pumped into a nearby stream.

Opening the door, Shrek realized the cottage was nothing more than a front office. A busy receptionist sat behind a big desk, scribbling away. He didn't greet Shrek and his companions as they entered.

"Hi. I'm here to see the . . ."

"The Fairy Godmother. I'm sorry," the receptionist said, without looking up. "She isn't in."

Just then, the intercom buzzed, and a voice said, "Jerome! Coffee and a Monte Cristo. Now!"

"Yes, Fairy Godmother, right away." Jerome the receptionist sighed, then noticed Shrek's stare. "Look, she's not seeing any clients today, okay?"

Jerome pushed a button on the intercom. "Humphries?"

"Yes, Jerome?" came the response on the other end.

"It's snack time . . . again," Jerome said sarcastically into the intercom, before looking up again. "Now, if you'd like to make an appointment . . ."

Shrek and company had gone. Jerome hadn't seen them walk out.

"Ugh," said Jerome. Good riddance! The big green one was ugly, anyway.

Inside the enormous magical potions factory, machinery mixed, mushed, and mashed ingredients in big vats, while elves scurried around, busily working.

Shrek and company took it all in. They watched from a catwalk up above. They had climbed there after sneaking in. From this vantage point, Shrek spotted the Fairy Godmother's office on the far side. They crept over.

Inside, the Fairy Godmother was levitating ingredients through the air with her wand. She was working over a smaller vat, pouring drips and drabs of the ingredients inside.

"Ooh, ooh!" the Fairy Godmother cooed excitedly. "A

drop of desire . . . a pinch of passion . . . and just a hint of . . . lust!"

The potion bubbled forth a large pink heart. The heart rose out of the vat and exploded with sparkling magic. The Fairy Godmother laughed and flapped her wings with joy. The pink heart dissipated and revealed Shrek.

"Eh, excuse me?"

The Fairy Godmother spun around to find Shrek, Donkey, and Puss standing there.

"What in Grimm's name are you doing here?" she demanded.

Shrek got right to the point. "Well, it seems that Fiona's not exactly happy."

"Oh?" the Fairy Godmother smirked.

The Fairy Godmother pretended to think seriously about it for a moment.

"And there's some question as to why that is?" she said mockingly. "Hmmm. Let's explore that, shall we?"

The Fairy Godmother reached for a book and thumbed through it. "Princess Cinderella — lived happily ever after. Oh, no ogre! Snow White — a handsome prince. No ogre! Sleeping Beauty — no ogres! Thumbelina? No. The Golden Bird, the Little Mermaid, Pretty Woman — no, no, no, no, NO! Ogres, you see, don't have happily ever afters!"

"All right, look lady!" Shrek exclaimed, pointing at her.

"Don't you point those dirty green sausages at me!" the Fairy Godmother screeched.

Shrek's nostrils flared angrily but before he could reply, the elf, Humphries, burst into the room.

"Your Monte Cristo and coffe —" he began. "Oh . . . sorry."

But Shrek had an idea.

"Ah, that's okay. We were just leaving. Very sorry to have wasted your time, Miss Godmother," Shrek said.

"Just go." The Fairy Godmother sneered.

"C'mon, guys," Shrek said, motioning Puss and Donkey to follow him.

Shrek looked across the factory floor. His eyes fell upon a door that was marked POTION CONTAINMENT ROOM. He smiled. Donkey didn't like the look of Shrek's smile one tiny bit.

A short time later, Humphries was walking past the janitor's closet. When the elf was within reach, a green fist grabbed him and pulled him into the closet. After a slight struggle, Shrek came out pushing a cart and wearing the elf's clothes as a disguise. He crossed the factory floor, heading for the Potion Containment Room. He had to pass a squad of security elves who carried bows and arrows. As Shrek approached, they glanced up at him.

"TGIF, hey, buddy?" Shrek said casually, and continued on.

At the Potion Containment Room, Shrek opened the door and quickly pushed the cart inside.

"Hey, man, you want to get your fine Corinthian footwear out of my face?" Donkey's voice came from inside the cart. "Man, that stinks."

"Well, you don't exactly smell like a basket of roses," Puss retorted.

Shrek turned the cart on its side and dumped his companions out. The room's walls were lined with shelves — impossibly tall shelves, filled with hundreds, maybe thousands, of different magical potions. Each potion was in a tiny, labeled bottle.

"Well, one of these has got to help," Shrek said optimistically.

"Ah! I was just concocting this very plan!" Puss stepped forward and pointed a paw into the air. "Already our minds are becoming one."

"Whoa, whoa, whoa!" Donkey stepped between them and looked at Puss. "Listen, if we need an expert on licking ourselves, we'll give you a call."

Donkey turned to look up at Shrek while clearing his throat. "Shrek, this is a bad idea."

Shrek wasn't listening. "Donkey, make yourself useful and go keep watch, will ya? Puss, do you think you could get to those bottles on top?"

"No problema, boss!" Puss saluted and lunged up a shelf.

"In one of my nine lives I was the great cat burglar of Santiago de Compostela. Ha ha ha ha ha!"

"Shrek, are you off your nut?" Donkey was incredulous.

"Donkey, keep watch!" Shrek commanded.

Donkey couldn't believe it. Not only did he think Shrek was crazy for wanting to become a handsome prince just to make Fiona's parents happy — and asking for big trouble messing with the Fairy Godmother — but now Shrek was trusting that crazy cat. Meanwhile he was being shuffled off to do guard duty. It was insulting! Donkey was supposed to be the best friend. Granted, Donkey wasn't very good at climbing shelves, but that was beside the point!

"Keep watch," Donkey muttered. "Yeah, I'm gonna keep watch. I'm gonna watch that Wicked Witch come down here and whammy-zammy a world of hurt all up your backside, that's what I'm gonna watch . . . and I'm gonna laugh, too!"

Shrek called up to Puss, who was way up top, "What do you see?"

"'Toad Stool Softener,'" Puss read one of the labels.

Donkey was watching them. "Oh, yeah, you're right! This is a good idea. I'm sure that is the perfect solution to marital problems."

"'Elf-A-Seltzer . . . Knight Quill,'" Puss continued.

"Try under 'H' for handsome," Shrek suggested.

Puss looked around. "Sorry, no 'Handsome.' How about 'Happily Ever After'?"

"What does it do?" Shrek asked.

Puss glanced at the label. "It says, 'Beauty divine . . .'"

"You know, in some cultures, Donkeys are revered as the wisest of all creatures," Donkey huffed, not paying attention to the door. "Especially us talking donkeys."

"Donkey, shut it!" Shrek growled.

Looking past Donkey, through the slightly open door, Shrek realized with alarm that Donkey had failed in his assigned duty. Several security guards, notching their arrows to bows, were headed in their direction!

"Quick, Puss!" Shrek called up to the cat. "We've got company!"

CHAPTER 11

"Hurry, Puss! Hurry up!" Shrek urged.

Puss grabbed the potion, knocking over several other bottles. Then he lost his grip on the bottle and both he and the potion fell. Donkey sprinted forward, dove, and caught the bottle in his mouth just before it smashed on the floor.

Puss landed on his feet next to Donkey and grinned. "Finally a good use for your mouth!" he said.

Just then an alarm went off and lights began flashing; a heavy security gate started to descend in front of the door — and Donkey swallowed the bottle of potion!

With no time to think, Shrek grabbed Donkey and Puss and made a run for the exit. They dove under the door, making it out just before the gate slammed down. They were back in the main potion room. Security elves ran toward them. There was nowhere to go! Shrek picked up Donkey and Puss and ran back to the large, bubbling cauldron. Jumping up next to it, he pushed it over. The boiling potion spilled out over the surprised guards.

Shrek leapt up into the air and grabbed hold of a hook on a pulley. Swinging his legs, he propelled himself across the length of the factory, the hook gliding swiftly along a sturdy cable.

Donkey glanced back at the chaos behind them, as the wave of potion washed past the guards and over test animals in their cages. Elves were turning into doves everywhere.

When Shrek reached the end of the cable, he let go, and as they landed, the bottle of potion popped out of Donkey's mouth. Shrek scooped it up and the three ran off into the forest.

The Fairy Godmother was furious when she got the whole story sorted out moments later. She surveyed the damage Shrek had left in his wake. The place was a shambles, and elves were scurrying around cleaning things up.

"I don't care whose fault it is, just get this place cleaned up!" she bellowed.

"Yes, Godmother!" the elves replied.

"And somebody bring me something deep-fried and smothered in chocolate!"

Just then, Prince Charming appeared and stalked over to his mother.

"Mother?" the prince said.

"Charming, sweetheart, oh, this isn't a good time, pump-kin," the Fairy Godmother replied, shooing him away. "Mama's working."

Prince Charming suddenly noticed the mess surrounding them. "What happened here?" he asked.

"The ogre, that's what!" the Fairy Godmother replied.

Charming drew his sword, prepared to fight. "Where is he, Mum? I shall rend his head from his shoulders! He will rue the very day he stole my kingdom from me!"

"Oh, put it away, junior! We're going to have to come up with something smarter than that," the Fairy Godmother said irritably.

Just then a dove approached with a clipboard, which he gave to the Fairy Godmother.

"Everything is accounted for, Fairy Godmother, except for one bottle of potion," the elf-dove reported.

The Fairy Godmother looked at the report. When she saw what potion they'd taken, a slow, nasty smile spread across her face.

"I do believe we can make this work to our advantage," she chuckled malevolently.

Meanwhile, in a nearby part of the forest, Shrek and his companions stopped to rest. Shrek pulled out the potion bottle and began to read the label. "'Happily Ever After potion, maximum strength. For you and your true love. Drink of this potion and bliss will be thine. Happiness, comfort, and beauty divine.'"

Donkey shook his head worriedly and clucked his tongue. "This don't feel right, Shrek. My Donkey senses are tingling all over! So, why don't you drop that jug o' voodoo and let's get out of here?"

"Look, it says 'beauty divine.'" Shrek held the bottle in Donkey's face, causing Donkey to go cross-eyed. "How bad can it be?"

Shrek pulled the cork out of the bottle and sniffed in the fumes. Immediately, he bent over and sneezed on a toadstool.

"See, look at that!" Donkey was riled. "You're already having an allergic reaction! See if Fiona thinks you're a hunk when you're all covered in bumps and lumps and stuff!"

As Donkey ranted, none of them noticed the toadstool Shrek sneezed on had started to sizzle and smoke.

Puss stepped forward. "Boss, just in case there is something wrong with the potion, allow me to take the first sip. It would be an honor to lay my life on the line for you."

"No, no, no! I don't think so!" Donkey jumped in, not wanting to be upstaged by the cat again. "If there's gonna be any animal testing here, I'm gonna do it! That's the best friend's job. Now, gimme that bottle!"

Donkey snatched the bottle and took a few swigs. *Glug! Glug! Glug!*

Anxiously, they leaned in and waited for a reaction. Moments passed without anything happening.

"Donkey? How do you feel?" Shrek asked.

"Uh, well . . . I don't feel any different." Donkey considered. "Do I look any different?"

"You still look like a jackass to me," said Puss.

"Huh." Shrek took the bottle back. "Maybe it doesn't work on donkeys."

Shrek was thoughtful for a moment. Presently, he shrugged and made a toast to the sky.

"Well, here's to us, Fiona." Shrek started to take a drink.

"Shrek!" Donkey stopped him. "You drink that, and there's no going back."

"I know." Shrek nodded.

"No more wallowing in the mud!" Donkey reminded him.

"I know! But I love Fiona more." Shrek glanced at the potion defiantly.

With that, Shrek took a big gulp of the potion.

"Shrek!"

Almost instantly, storm clouds gathered. The wind began to blow, the sky turned dark, a rumble was heard in the distance, and . . .

And . . .

Shrek passed wind again. Loudly.

"Ooh, Shrek." Donkey waved his hoof in front of his face and wrinkled his nose. "I think you grabbed the 'Farty Ever After' potion!"

"Maybe it's a dud," Puss suggested.

Shrek sagged with disappointment. "Maybe Fiona and I were never meant to be."

Lightning flashed and thunder roared. The sky broke open and rain poured down upon them. Donkey had been so distracted by Shrek's disappointment that he now thought the storm was some terrible magic.

"Oh, no! What did I tell you?" Donkey cried. "I think I feel something coming on! Oh, sweet sister, mother of mercy! I'm melting! I'm melting!"

"It's just the rain, Donkey," sighed Shrek sadly.

It was really pouring. Shrek and Puss ran for cover. Donkey looked up at the sky, and after a moment, followed them, embarrassed.

They were gone, and none of them had noticed that the toadstool that Shrek had sneezed on had transformed into a beautiful rose.

CHAPTER 12

They found a dry barn where they could wait out the storm. To pass the time, Shrek stared at the castle in the distance.

Donkey came and sat next to him. Shrek smiled sadly and gave Donkey a pat on the head.

"Aww, Shrek, don't worry, things just seem bad 'cause it's dark and rainy . . . and Fiona's father hired a sleazy hit man to whack you," Donkey said as Puss hissed at him.

"It'll be better in the morning," Donkey continued, ignoring the annoyed cat. "You'll see . . . the sun will come out . . . tomorrow . . . bet your bottom . . ."

Suddenly, Donkey's head got woozy. His legs began to wobble.

Shrek stared at Donkey who was twirling around. Suddenly, Donkey slumped to the ground, out cold.

"Donkey!" Shrek cried.

A wave of dizziness then passed over Shrek. He reached

out to grab something to steady himself, but grasped only thin air. He teetered and began to keel over.

Too late, Puss became aware of the shadow looming over him. He took his eyes off Donkey and looked up just in time to see Shrek come crashing down on top of him.

Lightning crackled in the sky outside. The light blasted bright, then grew dim. In the twilight, a puff of magical blue smoke burst through the barn doors and windows.

At the same time, Fiona was joining her parents in front of the castle's massive fireplace. The friendly crackle of the fire almost drowned out the sound of the cold rain outside.

"There you are!" The King smiled. "We missed you at dinner."

"What is it, darling?" the Queen asked, noticing the look on Fiona's face.

Fiona took a deep breath. This wasn't going to be easy. "Dad, I've been thinking about what you said. I'm going to set things right."

"Ah, excellent!" the King chuckled, misreading her. "That's my girl!"

Fiona continued, "It was a mistake to bring Shrek here. I know that now. I'm going out to find him, and then we're going back to the swamp where we belong."

It was then that her parents realized that Fiona had packed her bags. She picked them up and walked away.

The Queen and the King followed after her.

"Fiona, please," the Queen pleaded.

Fiona opened the front door.

"Let's not be rash, darling." The King panicked. "You can't go anywhere right now."

Fiona gave her parents one last look, turned, and was about to walk out into the driving rain.

"Fiona!" the Queen cried.

The princess took only a few steps before a huge gust of wind whipped up, sending rain-soaked leaves spinning around her. Just like Shrek and Donkey, Fiona became suddenly dizzy. She lost her balance and fainted.

A short while later, her parents had tucked her in bed with a warm comforter over her. Once she'd done all she could for her daughter, the Queen gave the King an icy glare and left the room.

The King lingered for a moment, looking forlornly at his daughter. He hoped that she would be okay. Soon he left, just missing the puff of magical blue smoke that burst in through the bedroom windows.

Hours passed and so did the storm. The sun came up on a beautiful morning. Birds twittered happily and fluffy white clouds floated in the sky.

Inside the barn, Shrek stretched and rolled over. He opened and closed his mouth. He rubbed his nose. He sat up, yawned, scratched his chest, and finally opened his eyes.

"Good morning, sleepy head!" A pretty young maid was right in his face.

"Aarrrgh!" Shrek yelled.

Two other maidens joined the first. They were all stunningly beautiful.

"Good morning!" said the second maid.

"We love your kitty!" The third maid was holding Puss and stroking him gently. The cat was loving it.

Shrek realized he had a terrible headache. "Owww! My head!"

"Here, I fetched you a pail of water." The first maid smiled.

"Ah . . . thanks." Shrek grabbed the pail, then screamed again.

His hands weren't fat and green anymore. They were long, slender, and *human*-looking. He quickly looked at his reflection in the water.

"Arghhh!" Shrek screamed for a third time. "A cute button nose? Thick wavy locks? I'm . . . I'm . . ."

"Gorgeous!" squealed the maidens.

I've turned into a human, thought Shrek. *And a handsome human, at that!*

"I'm Jill," said the maiden who'd fetched the pail of water, presumably from up a hill somewhere. "What's your name?"

"Um . . . Shrek."

"Shrek? Wow!" Jill grinned and started massaging Shrek's shoulders. "Are you from Europe? You're so tense."

"I want to rub his shoulders!" cried one of the other girls.

"I've got it covered, thanks." Jill scowled at her.

Shrek wasn't used to this kind of attention. Usually girls who looked like Jill and her friends screamed and ran from him. Sometimes they fainted. They most certainly did not rub his shoulders. This was . . . kind of nice. He could get used to this.

Wait! What was he saying? He shook his head and came to his senses.

"Have you ladies seen my donkey?"

"Who are you calling Donkey?" a familiar voice asked.

Shrek turned and his mouth fell open. "Donkey! You're a . . . a . . ."

Donkey was standing in the doorway. Only now he was a noble white steed, rimmed with golden sunlight.

"I'm a stallion, baby!" Donkey exclaimed.

CHAPTER 13

Shrek was having a hard time believing what had happened. Donkey, however, had no trouble at all accepting his new appearance.

"Look, Shrek!" Donkey cried. "I can whinny. I can count."

Donkey whinnied and tapped his hoof four times on the ground. He began to trot around the barn.

"Look at me, Shrek, I'm trotting! That's some quality potion! What's in that stuff?"

Puss mocked Donkey while smiling playfully.

"'Oooh, don't take that potion, Mr. Boss! It's veeeeery baaad!' Pfft!"

Puss picked up the potion bottle and read from the label, "'Warning: side effects may include burning, itching, oozing, weeping. Not intended for heart patients or those with nervous disorders.'"

Nervous disorders? Puss and Shrek watched Donkey carefully.

"I'm trottin', I'm trottin', I'm trottin' in place! Yeah!" Donkey capered about until he noticed his friends staring at him. "What?"

Puss turned his attention back to the label. "Señor! 'To make the effects of this potion permanent, the drinker must obtain his true love's kiss by midnight.'"

"Midnight?" Shrek's handsome face frowned. "Why is it always midnight?"

"Ooh, pick me!" one of the maidens ran up and dropped at Shrek's feet. "I'll be your true love!"

"No, I will!" cried Jill, who came tumbling after.

Shrek held out his hands. "Look, ladies, I already have a true love."

"Oh!" came the disappointed response.

"And take it from me, boss, you are going to have one satisfied princess!" Puss purred.

Donkey wanted to make sure Shrek didn't get too full of himself.

"Hey, let's face it — you may be a lot easier on the eyes, but inside, you're still the same old, mean, salty . . ."

"Easy . . ." Shrek warned.

". . . cantankerous, stanky, foul . . ."

Shrek looked a bit annoyed. "All right, then."

". . . angry ogre you've always been," Donkey finished.

"And you're still the same annoying donkey!" Shrek replied.

Donkey nodded with a smile, his golden mane flowing. "Yeah."

Shrek paused and considered this for a moment.

"Well, I sure hope she likes the new me."

Shrek raised his arms and turned around to show himself off. His ogre pants dropped off his svelte new physique, leaving him standing only in his long tunic. The three maidens giggled as Shrek turned red with embarrassment.

"Aha. Well, first things first," Donkey said. "We need to get you out of those ogre clothes."

A few minutes later, Shrek, Donkey, and Puss were hiding behind a boulder next to a road. They watched as a fancy, horse-drawn carriage rounded the bend and approached.

"Ready?" asked Shrek.

"Ready!" came Donkey and Puss's reply.

As the carriage passed, it rolled over something in the road.

"Owwww!" Donkey cried.

A nobleman leaned out of the carriage window and shouted, "Driver, stop!"

The driver pulled the reins and the carriage came to a stop. The nobleman, a short, chubby fellow, opened the door and looked back to see what the carriage had rolled over. He gasped.

Donkey was lying in the road, pretending to be in serious pain.

"Oh, my! Help me, please!" Donkey was hamming it up, big time. "My racing days are over! I'm blind! I'm blind! Tell me the truth, will I ever be able to play the violin again?"

The nobleman ran to him. "You poor creature! Is there anything I can do for you?"

"Well . . ." Donkey smiled. "I guess there is *one* thing."

Puss jumped out from behind Donkey and pointed his sword. "Take off your powdered wig and step away from your drawers!"

The stunned nobleman slowly took off his wig and dropped it on the ground. A few minutes later, Shrek was dressed in the nobleman's clothing and plopping the wig on his head. Although Shrek was a lot smaller in his human form, he still had to stuff himself into the nobleman's clothes, as they were several sizes too small for him. He looked ridiculous.

"Not bad," Puss fibbed.

"Not bad at all," concurred Donkey.

Donkey and Puss looked at each other and burst out laughing. "Bwah-ha-ha-ha-ha!"

Shrek gave them an annoyed look and pulled a fake mole off his cheek. This was hopeless!

About that time, the nobleman's somewhat-slow son leaned out of the carriage.

"I say, Father?" the son called. "Is everything all right? Father?"

The son got out of the carriage. He wore a very princely outfit and was exactly the same size as Shrek in his new form.

Shrek, Donkey, and Puss smiled.

Moments later, father and son stood in their undergarments as Shrek, in his new wardrobe, mounted his trusty horse, Donkey, and bade them farewell.

"Thank you!" Shrek waved as Puss jumped atop Donkey to ride, too. "You have done a very noble deed!"

With that, Donkey reared up, bucked Puss off, and took off like a shot, galloping over hill and dale, carrying Shrek back to the castle. Puss picked himself up and chased after them, cursing at Donkey in Spanish.

CHAPTER 14

This time when Shrek and Donkey rode into the kingdom of Far Far Away, the experience was much better.

Women in bistros looked up from their coffees. Male commuters turned to stare.

Shrek caught his reflection in a shop window. He really did cut a dashing figure riding Donkey, his noble steed.

Farmers delivering goods to market beamed as he passed. Young maidens fawned in his presence. When he smiled, the sun sparkled off his pearly-white teeth just so.

Of course, Donkey and Puss got their share of attention, too. Puss flirted and Donkey tossed his mane like he was a beauty contestant.

At the royal palace, Shrek addressed the attentive guards. "Tell Princess Fiona her husband, Sir Shrek, is here to see her."

One of the guards ran into the palace as fast as his steel-plated legs would carry him. It seemed the command of a handsome nobleman was to be obeyed promptly.

Inside the castle, Fiona was just getting out of bed. She yawned and stretched and made her way to the vanity. She poured some water from a pitcher into her wash basin, grabbed a hand towel, and washed her face. Using another towel to dry off, she blinked and looked at her reflection in the mirror.

She was human again . . . and beautiful.

Her jaw dropped. She blinked to make sure she wasn't imagining things. She wasn't.

"Eeeeeeeeeeeeeeeeeeeeeeek!" Fiona screamed.

Outside the castle, Shrek heard the princess scream and jumped into action.

"Fiona!"

He dismounted and ran into the castle.

Fiona was still staring at herself in the mirror when she heard Shrek call her name.

"Shrek?" Quickly, she ran out to find him.

Well on his way to Fiona's room, Shrek heard her voice coming from a room he'd just passed.

"Shrek!"

Puzzled, Shrek went into the room. He'd never been in this room before. But there, standing in front of the window, was a silhouetted, hooded figure that could have been the princess.

"Fiona?"

Shrek sensed something was wrong. He looked at the

figure's feet — but the feet weren't touching the ground! The figure discarded the hooded cloak and revealed herself. It was the Fairy Godmother, flying a few inches off the floor to make herself seem about Fiona's height. Shrek took a step back.

The Fairy Godmother smiled like a shark. "Hello, handsome," she said.

"You?" Shrek scowled. "Where's Fiona?"

Realizing that she had deliberately tricked him, he turned to run out of the room shouting, "Fiona! Fiona!"

An enchanted dresser, vanity, and other menacing furniture were blocking his way out.

"You wanna dance, pretty boy?" sneered the dresser.

Down in the courtyard, Donkey and Puss were still waiting when Fiona ran out of the palace.

"Princess!" Donkey cried, surprised to see her in her human form.

Fiona recognized Donkey's voice, but was stunned to see him as a horse. "Donkey?"

Donkey grinned. "Wow, the potion worked on you, too, huh?"

"What potion?" Fiona asked.

"It's kind of a long story," Donkey said, kicking the dirt absently with one hoof. "But, see, Shrek and I took some magic potion, and, well . . . now we're sexy!"

Fiona was beyond stunned. Her eyes fell on Puss, who

was sitting on Donkey's back, cleaning himself. Puss stopped when he noticed Fiona. He was enchanted by her beauty.

"Shrek?" Fiona asked.

Puss raised his eyebrows. "For you, I could be."

"Yeah, you wish!" Donkey scoffed.

Fiona was getting impatient. "Donkey, where is Shrek?"

"He just went inside looking for you!"

She ran back into the castle. She needed to see Shrek as soon as possible. Something wasn't right, and she wanted to make sure he was okay.

"Shrek? Shrek?"

"Fiona . . ." came a voice from the darkness of a room beside her.

She entered the room. A silhouetted man was standing out on the balcony. She moved toward him. Could this handsome man really be her ogre? She looked at him carefully, studying his face.

"Shrek? What happened to your voice?"

Prince Charming smiled at her. "Well, the potion changed a lot of things, but not the way I feel about you."

Just then, the Queen and King ran in, awakened by all the yelling. When they saw that their daughter was human again, they gasped.

"Fiona!" exclaimed the Queen. "It's . . . it's you!"

"Charming . . . ?" the King asked, quietly.

Prince Charming stepped up to the King and Queen with a ridiculously wide grin on his face.

"Mum! Dad! It's me, *Shrek*," Prince Charming lied, staring pointedly at the King. "I know you never get a second chance at a first impression, but what do you think?"

The King hesitated for just a second. He knew the truth, but finally he smiled, going along with the lying prince.

In another part of the castle, Shrek was watching Fiona, the King, the Queen, and some handsome stranger — probably a prince — talking. The Fairy Godmother had Shrek watching through a window. Shrek observed the pantomime as the stranger hugged Fiona, while the King patted the prince on the back. The Queen beamed happily, and Fiona — his Fiona, back in human form — kept looking at the handsome man with an amazed little smile.

"Fiona!" Shrek cried, pounding on the window.

"Oh, shoot," said the Fairy Godmother in a mocking tone. "I don't think they can hear us, pigeon."

Shrek continued to stare, his heart close to breaking.

"Don't you think you've already messed her life up enough?" the Fairy Godmother asked.

"I only wanted her to be happy," Shrek said, sadly.

The Fairy Godmother's smile was devoid of any warmth. "And now she can be. Oh, sweetheart, look at her. She's finally found the prince of her dreams. It's time you stop living in a fairy tale, Shrek. She's a princess and you're an ogre. That's something no amount of potion is going to change."

Shrek watched as Prince Charming led Fiona away.

"If you really love her, you'll let her be," the Fairy God-mother finished.

CHAPTER 15

Having watched the dreadful image of his one true love with another man, Shrek didn't waste any time leaving the castle. With Donkey and Puss following behind him, wondering what was going on, Shrek walked back into the city. He headed for the seediest bar he could find.

The place was called The Poison Apple and it was the pits. A pirate captain, who had a hook at the end of one arm, played a song on the piano, and various fairy-tale villains whispered together at tables — while keeping a close eye on two knights who were sitting at another table eating doughnuts.

Shrek, Donkey, and Puss sat at the bar. The bartender, one of Cinderella's ugly stepsisters named Doris, poured drinks.

"There you go, boys," Doris said.

Puss threw a coin on the bar. "Just leave the bottle."

"Hey, why the long face?" Doris asked.

"I never should have rescued her from that tower in the first place," Shrek said, sadly.

"I hate Mondays!" Puss groused.

Donkey ignored Puss and turned to Shrek. "I can't believe that you're just gonna walk away from the best thing that ever happened to you."

"What choice do I have?" Shrek asked. "She loves that pretty boy, Prince Charming."

"He's gorgeous!" Doris sighed.

"But I don't get it, Shrek," Donkey said, now ignoring Doris. "You love Fiona."

"Which is why I should just walk away," Shrek said, staring down at the bar.

Just then the door burst open and a cloaked figure entered the room. It was the King in disguise. He glanced around the bar, but didn't recognize Shrek or Donkey in their new forms. He sidled up to the bar and beckoned to Doris.

"Uhmmm, excuse me, I'm here for . . ." he whispered.

"The secret meeting?" Doris asked, loudly.

The King looked nervously around and then nodded. Doris gestured toward a door in the back of the room. Two of the Fairy Godmother's goons stood in front of it and glared at the King as he slipped past them.

Shrek, Donkey, and Puss exchanged curious glances, then quickly got up and snuck outside.

CHAPTER 16

Shrek, Donkey, and Puss found a window through which they could see into the backroom.

The Fairy Godmother and Prince Charming were there, and obviously waiting for the King.

The King smiled nervously at the pair as he entered the room.

"You better have a good reason for dragging us down here, Harold," the Fairy Godmother said.

"Yes, yes of course . . . the castle's a bit risky, and Lillian's a little suspicious . . . perhaps it's best if we just call the whole thing off," the King stammered out. "It's just that . . . well, Fiona isn't warming up to Prince Charming."

"Um, FYI, not my fault," Prince Charming popped into the conversation. "I mean, how charming can I be when I have to pretend I'm that dreadful ogre?"

"It's nobody's fault," the King said, quickly. "I mean, you can't force someone to fall in love."

"I do it all the time." The Fairy Godmother reached into

her dress and pulled out a bottle of magic potion, which she handed to the King. "Have Fiona drink this and she'll fall in love with the first man she kisses."

The King looked at the bottle, then squared his shoulders. "No," he said. "I won't do it."

Suddenly, the Fairy Godmother was right in his face. She pressed her wand against his nose, then began to speak.

"I seem to recall how I once helped *you* acquire a happy ending of your own," she said. "And I can take it all away just as easily. Is that what you want? Is it? Hmm?"

"No," the King said, weakly.

"Good boy." The Fairy Godmother was all sweetness now. "We have to go. . . . I said I'd do Charming's hair before the ball."

"Oh, thank you, Mother," Prince Charming gushed.

"*Mother!*" Donkey cried from outside.

". . . un . . . Mary! A talking horse!" Shrek cried, trying to cover up Donkey's outburst.

The Fairy Godmother turned to the window and saw Shrek, Donkey, and Puss peering in. "The ogre!" she cried, racing out of the bar as Donkey ran around the corner. But then her eyes fell on some knights. She had an idea.

"Thieves! Bandits! Stop them!" she cried.

The knights grabbed their weapons and helmets and took off after the trio.

CHAPTER 17

Shrek and his buddies were arrested by the armored constables. They struggled and tried to explain what was going on, but to no avail.

They were fingerprinted, photographed, and hung in shackles on the jail wall. As evening came on, Shrek hung grimly. He was afraid that before midnight, Fiona would kiss Prince Charming and be lost to him forever.

Meanwhile, back at Shrek's shack in the swamp, the fairy-tale folk who were house-sitting were crowded around the magic mirror watching the start of the royal ball. Everyone was anxious to get a glimpse of Shrek, Fiona, and Donkey.

At the palace, guests for the ball were starting to arrive. On the red carpet, a gossip mirror broadcast images of the glitzy and the glamorous as they exited their stretch-carriages and entered the castle. A loud-mouthed female court announcer critiqued what the guests were wearing, although no one really knew what made her such an expert.

"Oh!" the announcer was reporting. "And who's this, who's this . . . who is this? It's the Fairy Godmother!"

The Fairy Godmother stepped out of her carriage and waved to her fans.

"Hello, Far Far Away! Oh, kisses, kisses, kisses!" she cried as her bodyguards picked her up and carried her down the red carpet.

The red carpet image faded to be replaced by the ME TV logo and a promise to be right back with more of the excitement.

For his part, Gingerbread Man was bored to tears. "Man! I hate these ball shows. Flip over to *Wheel of Torture!*"

"I'm not flipping anywhere, sir, until we see Shrek and Fiona," Pinocchio said sharply.

"Ah, whizzers on you guys," Gingerbread Man grumped. "Hey, mice, pass me a buffalo wing!"

The Three Blind Mice grabbed a wing and tossed it in Gingerbread Man's general direction, but it landed in the goldfish bowl and floated there with the dead fish.

"Nice shot," Gingerbread Man scowled.

The magic mirror went to a commercial break. "Tonight on *Knights* . . ."

Gingerbread Man's eyes lit up. "Now, here's a good show."

In the mirror, images flashed by of handsome Shrek and steed Donkey getting captured and arrested by armored men. None of their friends watching thought much of it at first, since Shrek and Donkey were in their handsome guises.

"Freeze!" ordered a knight, while other guards wrestled Donkey to the ground.

"That ain't necessary," Donkey was shouting. "Hey! Ow! Police brutality! Police brutality!"

"I have to talk to Princess Fiona!" cried Shrek, as the knights tried to shove him into a paddy wagon.

At the mention of the princess's name, Shrek's house guests stopped whatever they were doing and listened carefully.

"Stop struggling!" growled a knight.

"But . . ."

"We warned you!" said the knight, and he shook a pepper grinder at Shrek's face.

"Ow! My eyes!"

The paddy wagon pulled away, with Donkey yelling, "I'm not even a horse. I'm a donkey!"

"I'm her husband! Shrek!" the transformed ogre cried.

Every jaw dropped in Shrek's living room. All the fairy-tale creatures looked at one another.

The commercial over, the magic mirror returned to coverage of the royal ball.

Meanwhile, back at the castle, the King was preparing two mugs of tea, looking around now and then to make sure no one could see what he was doing. Somewhat reluctantly, he uncorked the bottle of magic potion the Fairy Godmother gave him and poured the contents into one of the mugs.

He carried the mugs on a tray up the back stairs to Fiona's room. All the while, he kept a close eye on the one with the magic potion, so as to not get the two mixed up. He softly knocked on his daughter's door.

"Darling?" he entered. "How about a nice hot cup of tea before the ball?"

Fiona wouldn't look at him. "I'm not going."

The King was shocked. He thought everything from here on out would be simple. A quick kiss. A magical enchantment. Happily ever after.

"But the whole kingdom's turned out to celebrate your marriage!"

From where she stood, Fiona could see Prince Charming down on the red carpet, posing for all the cameras.

"There's just one problem. That's not my husband! I mean, look at him!"

The King sat the tea tray on the bureau. "I grant you, he is a bit different. But people change for the ones they love."

The King looked at his reflection in the mirror, at his big eyes and wide mouth. He had more wrinkles these days. His was the face of a man who'd carried a secret for far too long, he thought.

"You'd be surprised how much I changed for your mother."

"Changed?" Fiona laughed, but without humor. "Shrek hasn't changed, he's completely lost his mind!"

The King went to her and gently took her slender hands in his wide ones. "Darling, why not come down to the ball and give him another chance? For me? You might find you like this new Shrek."

"But, it's the old one I fell in love with." She couldn't believe how different Shrek had become, and how quickly. "I'd give anything to have him back."

Hearing this, the King felt a pang of guilt. Fiona sadly let go of his hands and went to the bureau to get a mug of tea. Seeing this, the King panicked.

"Ah, darling!" he took the mug from her and offered her the other. "That's mine. Decaf. Otherwise, I'm up all night."

Fiona took the other, and the King anxiously watched her as she drank it.

CHAPTER 18

At the jailhouse, Donkey was raising a ruckus.

"Help us! I can't take it anymore!" Donkey bellowed, pulling at his shackles. "I gotta get out of here! Hey, what about my Miranda rights? You're supposed to say I have the right to remain silent. Nobody said I have the right to remain silent!"

"Donkey, you have the right to remain silent," Shrek said.

Puss threw back his head dramatically. "I must hold on, too, before I go totally mad!"

"Shrek? Donkey?"

Puss looked up at a grate in the ceiling. Pinocchio, Gingerbread Man, and the Three Blind Mice were up there.

"Too late," Puss sighed. "I have gone totally mad."

"Gingy! Pinocchio!" Shrek whispered excitedly. "Get us out of here!"

BOOM! The three pigs blew off the lock on the ceiling

grate. The fairy-tale creatures lowered Pinocchio down by his puppet strings through the opening.

But Pinocchio couldn't reach Shrek. The pigs swung his wooden body back and forth, but it was no use.

"Quick! Tell a lie," Gingerbread Man said as he slid down and landed on Pinocchio's nose.

"I cannot tell a lie," Pinocchio replied. But that was a lie. His nose grew, inching Gingerbread Man closer to Shrek.

"Tell another one," Gingerbread Man urged. "A bigger one."

"I told you that I cannot lie," Pinocchio insisted. And that was an even bigger lie. Pinocchio's nose grew until Ginerbread Man could easily reach Shrek's shackles and unlock them. Shrek fell to the ground. Puss was next and then Donkey.

Shrek rubbed his wrists and looked at Far Far Away through the small cell window.

"We have to stop that kiss!" he said.

"I thought you said you were going to walk away?" Donkey said.

"I was, but I can't let them do this to Fiona," Shrek replied.

Shrek studied the castle, then looked at Gingy. He was beginning to get an idea.

He turned to Gingy. "Do you know the Muffin Man?"

"Sure, he lives on Drury Lane," Gingerbread Man said matter-of-factly. "Why?"

"Because we're gonna need flour." Shrek's face glowed with determination. "Lots and lots of flour."

A short time later, a small boy sat on the steps of his house, eating an ice-cream cone. The evening was pleasant and there were people strolling down the lamp-lit avenue.

Suddenly, the ground began to shake violently and repeatedly, as if something huge was walking the boy's way. People panicked and started running for shelter. The vibration grew stronger and the boy lost hold of his frozen treat. He looked up, about to scream at the top of his lungs, but instead gasped with delight at what he saw.

A giant foot smashed down near him, sending him flying into the bushes. People who dared peek out their windows saw an awesome sight. In the middle of the street strode a gigantic Gingerbread Man, at least a hundred feet tall! Shrek rode on its shoulder. The normal-sized Gingerbread Man rode on Shrek's shoulder.

"Go, Mongo!" Gingerbread Man cried.

"There it is, Mongo! To the castle! Go!" Shrek shouted with a raised fist.

They had named the giant Mongo.

The Muffin Man created Mongo according to Shrek's specifications and brought it to life. They allowed Mongo to rise, and when the gargantuan was standing, Shrek commanded it to attack the castle. At first, it had been difficult to get the giant Gingerbread Man to focus, but Donkey had solved the problem.

"Mongo! Down here! Look at the pony! Dancing pony! Nice dancing pony! Follow the pretty pony! Pretty pony wants to play at the castle!" he shouted.

Immediately, Mongo, carrying Shrek and Gingerbread Man, began to follow Donkey toward the royal palace. Puss followed closely behind, along with the small army of fairy-tale folk.

CHAPTER 19

Fiona finally agreed to make an appearance at the ball. Trumpets sounded with regal flare as she stepped onto the landing of the grand stairway that led down to the packed ballroom.

"Ladies and gentlemen," a herald announced. "Presenting Princess Fiona and her new husband, Prince Shrek."

A spotlight illuminated Fiona. Moments later, Prince Charming emerged from the shadows to join her. They descended the stairs as the crowd cheered. The prince smiled broadly and waved to the audience.

"Shrek, what are you doing?" Fiona asked, knowing that Shrek usually hated crowds and attention. Heck, the old Shrek hated almost everything.

"I'm just playing the part, Fiona." His eyes sparkled as he leaned in for a kiss.

Fiona leaned away from him. "Is that glitter on your lips?"

"Cherry flavored."

Again, Prince Charming dive-bombed for a kiss, and Fiona

dodged him a second time. She was finding herself repulsed by him.

"What is it with you?" Fiona frowned.

The fact was, Fiona had to keep reminding herself that this was Shrek — her husband, her one true love.

Music began to play and Prince Charming gave her his most sincere look. "Fiona, my princess, would you honor me with a dance?" he cooed.

"Since when do you dance?" Fiona asked, wrinkling her nose.

"Fiona, my sweet, if there's one thing I know, it's that love is full of surprises."

The prince offered her his hand, gesturing to the dance floor. Under the spotlight as they were, everyone saw this. When Fiona appeared hesitant to dance with her handsome husband, the crowd started chanting, "Dance! Dance! Dance!"

Realizing there was no escape, Fiona reluctantly took Charming's hand and allowed him to lead her onto the dance floor. The attending guests' cheers were deafening.

In fact, the real Shrek could hear the cheers from outside, as he and his companions approached the castle.

"All right, big fella, let's crash this party!" Shrek ordered Mongo to begin the attack.

"Man the catapults!" cried the captain of the guard as he heard the thumping of the giant Gingerbread Man. "Ready? Fire!"

The catapult stones were lit afire and launched at the invaders. From his perch on Mongo's shoulder, Shrek noticed the fiery attack first.

"Incoming! Brace yourselves!" Shrek yelled.

A fireball hit Mongo squarely in the chest, knocking off one of his gumdrop buttons. Mongo stared at the button, then roared. Bending down, he picked up the gumdrop and kicked it at the castle walls.

"Incoming!" warned the captain of the guard, before the gumdrop hit the catapults, destroying them.

Shrek smiled. On his shoulder, Gingerbread Man hooted and cheered for his bigger, younger brother.

Shrek urged Mongo and his band of supporters forward. With thundering footsteps, Mongo took great strides and reached the castle moat. He jumped into the water just outside the raised castle drawbridge. He thrust his hands, burnt to a crispity-crunch after handling the fireball, into the cracks on either side of the drawbridge and got a good grip.

"Man the cauldrons!" came the captain's orders on the bulwark.

The guards hoisted a giant bottle of milk into the air and poured it into a gigantic cast-iron cauldron. Another guard swung a large, hot pipe into position inside the cauldron while others turned the crank to steam the milk. It took mere seconds for the milk to become boiling hot.

Down below, Shrek said to Mongo, "That's it! Heave!"

Mongo pulled at the closed drawbridge. It started to give way on the very first tug.

"Ho!" shouted the guards as they dumped the hot milk over the side.

Mongo's head was doused with the boiling liquid.

"Noooo!" Gingy cried.

But Mongo wasn't about to be defeated so easily. He ignored the pain and the big dollop of foam on his head that made it look like he had a hairdo.

On the battlements, the captain yelled angrily to his men, "More heat! Less foam!"

Mongo pulled the drawbridge again, causing it to buckle farther outward.

"Heave!" urged Shrek, starting to run up Mongo's arm toward the opening.

"Ho!" cried the captain, and once again boiling milk was poured over the side, this time with a lot less foam.

"Noooo!" bellowed Shrek as the gigantic cookie sank to his knees, then fell backward into the moat. His arms had broken off and remained in the cracks of the drawbridge, but they were dissolving quickly. Shrek realized that Mongo's arms wouldn't hold out much longer, so he dived through the crack between the drawbridge and the castle wall just before the drawbridge slammed back into place.

"Shrek!" Donkey yelled in alarm.

Shrek's friends looked on in horror. They couldn't tell if

he'd made it inside safely. But suddenly, the drawbridge clanged open. Shrek had lowered it!

"Come on!" Shrek called, urging his army forward.

"Yeah! Wahoo!" cheered Donkey and the fairy-tale folk as they ran into the castle.

Gingerbread Man stayed behind, standing on Mongo's face as the giant slowly melted into the moat.

"No, no, nooooo! Mongo!" Gingerbread Man cried.

Mongo looked at Gingerbread Man one last time and gave a little smile. "Beeee goooooooood . . ."

Mongo's head started sinking into the water, and it looked like Gingerbread Man was going to meet the same fate. But just as Gingy was about to hit the water, a sword reached down and swooped him up and out of danger. It was Puss, who had come back for him.

In the ballroom, the celebration continued. Everyone, except Fiona, was having a grand time. Even the King, dressed up in shining, clunky armor, was smiling as he hip-hopped with the Queen. No one was aware that a battle was raging outside, since the dance music was so loud.

Prince Charming spun Fiona across the dance floor, making her dizzy. He grabbed her around the waist and vigorously dipped her. Once more, he leaned in for a kiss, and since she was so dizzy, Fiona could do little to stop him.

His lips came closer, mere inches from hers. It looked as if nothing could stop him now.

CHAPTER 20

"Stop!" shouted a voice. "Back away from my wife!"

A hush fell over the crowd. Looking up, everyone stared in awe at the handsome stranger.

He was as good-looking as Fiona's husband, they thought, but seemed more noble somehow. He sat upon a handsome steed, making the most dashing of entrances.

"Shrek?" Fiona asked as he dismounted and approached.

People gasped. If this was Shrek, who was that chap wearing the lip glitter?

"This man is an imposter!" the Fairy Godmother cried.

"Yes, he's an imposter! I am the 'Shrek.' Isn't that right, Mummy?" Prince Charming said.

The Fairy Godmother was furious. She raised her wand, ready to send a blast at Shrek. But he stepped aside, revealing the Three Little Pigs.

"Now!" Shrek cried.

"Pigs in a blanket!" cried the First Little Pig, as his two brothers launched him out of a tablecloth at the Fairy Godmother. The pig grabbed her and hung on as the Fairy God-mother tried to shake him off.

"Pinocchio! Get the wand!" Shrek called.

Shrek swung Pinocchio around by his strings, then sent him flying toward the Fairy Godmother.

But the Fairy Godmother zapped Pinocchio with her wand, transforming him into flesh and blood.

"I'm a real boy!" Pinocchio cried in amazement, crashing hard into a banquet cart.

The Fairy Godmother finally managed to free herself from the pig, but before she could use the wand again, the Wolf inhaled deeply and blew. Fairy Godmother was spun around by the wind, and her wand flew out of her hand. One of the pigs set off after it, with the Fairy Godmother right behind him. The pig caught the wand, then quickly threw it to Donkey. The Fairy Godmother followed.

"Donkey!" Gingy cried.

Donkey threw the wand over the crowd toward Gingy, and once again the Fairy Godmother was in hot pursuit. Gingy caught the wand, then passed it to the Three Blind Mice, but they missed it. The wand landed on the ground and a magic burst hit Pinocchio, who was transformed back into a puppet.

Shrek dove for the wand, pushing it out of the way just as the Fairy Godmother reached for it. Suddenly, the wand was flipped into the air by a skillful sword. When it came down, Puss grabbed it.

"Pray for mercy, from Puss . . ." The cat smiled charmingly at the Fairy Godmother.

". . . and Donkey!" Donkey stood over her threateningly.

Seeing her opportunities slipping away, the Fairy Godmother yelled to Prince Charming, "Kiss her! Kiss her now!"

Fiona was slow to react, and the prince grabbed her. He planted a big kiss on her lips.

"Nooo!" Shrek cried in anguish.

A victorious smile spread across the Fairy Godmother's face. Now Fiona would love her son forever, no matter what.

The ballroom was silent. The King watched nervously. Fiona pulled out of Prince Charming's lip-lock. She looked dazed. To Shrek's horror, she stepped up to the prince and took his head lovingly into her hands.

Then she reared back and head-butted him so hard, Prince Charming crumpled into an unconscious heap.

Shrek and Fiona ran into each other's arms.

"Fiona!"

"Shrek!"

"Harold! You were supposed to give her the potion!"

"Oops!" The King gave a wry little smile. "I guess I served her the wrong tea."

With an angry wave of her hand, the magic wand flew

from Puss's grasp and back into hers. A huge thunderclap boomed, and lightning flashed all around.

The Fairy Godmother summoned up every ounce of her power, preparing for one massive magical attack on Shrek. As she rose off the ground, her face took on an eerie glow.

The King looked at his daughter, then at Shrek.

Just as the Fairy Godmother released her magic, Shrek pushed Fiona to safety.

But the King dived in front of Shrek, taking the blast full-on.

The wicked magic deflected off the King's shiny armor and bounced right back at the Fairy Godmother.

THOOM! The Fairy Godmother disappeared in a thunderous explosion. As the smoke cleared, all that was left were her glasses.

Fiona ran to where her father fell. All she saw was his empty, smoking armor. The fairy-tale folk, including Gingerbread Man, joined her, looking down sadly.

Tears filled her eyes. "Is he . . ."

Gingerbread Man bent closer to the armor. "Yup. He croaked."

Out from a crack in the armor came a frog. "Ribbit."

The Queen approached. "Harold?"

"Dad?" Fiona exclaimed.

The King, now a frog, looked at the sea of faces staring at him, then turned back to Fiona.

"Fiona, I'd hoped you'd never see me like this," the King said, his tongue shooting out a bit.

Donkey looked at Shrek. "Man! And he gave *you* a hard time."

"Donkey."

"No, no, no. He's right." The King hopped over to Shrek. "I'm sorry to both of you. I only wanted what was best for Fiona. But I can see now she already has it."

Shrek nodded.

The Queen picked the King up. "Harold."

"I'm sorry, Lillian, for everything. I just wish I could be the man you deserve."

Tears of love were in her eyes. "You're more a man today than you ever were . . . warts and all."

Everyone laughed politely. The clock began to chime midnight.

"Midnight!" Shrek cried. "Fiona, is this what you want? If you kiss me now, we'll stay this way forever."

"You'd do that, for me?" Fiona asked quietly.

"Yes," Shrek said.

Fiona looked at him, then at her parents, then back at him.

"I want what any princess wants . . . to live happily ever after . . ." Fiona came into Shrek's arms. He bent to kiss her. ". . . with the ogre I married." Fiona stopped his kiss.

As the clock neared its last chime, Shrek smiled at Fiona gratefully. She really did love the ogre inside him.

"Whatever happens, I must not cry!" Puss bit his paw as tears welled up. "You cannot make me cry!"

The last chime sounded. Fiona and Shrek held each other tightly as the transformation began, lifting and spinning them high into the air. Strange light shot out of their bodies. The crowd stared as Donkey, too, was lifted up and changed. When they all landed softly, they were back to their former selves.

"Now, where were we?" Fiona said.

"Oh, I remember," Shrek answered.

He dipped Fiona and spun around with her in a silent dance. He held her tenderly and kissed her.

The crowd cheered and Donkey whistled.

"Hey!" Puss admonished everyone good-naturedly. "Isn't we supposed to be having a fiesta?"

"Yeah," agreed Donkey, cueing the band to start the music again. "Uno, dos, cuatro!"

The party lasted well into the night. It was the most amazing celebration, mainly because Fiona and Shrek were together again, but also because the people of the kingdom of Far Far Away accepted them for the ogres they were.

Shrek's heart was brimming with happiness. He was sure that now they would live happily ever after.

Wouldn't they?

THE END